FOR *the* SAKE *of my* EGO

Ajay Setia

Harleen Walia

Invincible Publishers

First published in India in 2017 by Invincible Publishers

ISBN: 978-81-93238-24-0

Invincible Publishers
G - 120, Sushant Lok III, Sector 57, Gurgaon-122002

Opposite Kasturba Ashram, Radaur Distt Yamuna Nagar, Haryana- 135133

Digitally Printed at Replika Press Pvt. Ltd.

First the real good ones!

I thank Harleen Walia, the girl who has beautified my words and gave my thoughts a horizon that could form story.

And for keeping cool at all the times I get mad.

I would thank Mom and Dad for being an unmoved support and blessing me with their trust at every moment that passes us by. God for giving me experiences that I loved being a part of, the best amongst which is this book. Life without you people would have meant deficient.

Acknowledgements are not always about the brighter side.

I have list too long to name here of people who have cut me down for ever. Though, all those bitter things hardly made a difference, but they do form a part of my first book. But all those out there, please don't devalue our efforts by taking this as my answer.

Ajay Setia

This is the part that I eagerly awaited to write!

My first thanks would go to the invisible man in the boundless sky for writing wonderful stories an insignificant fraction of which we sometimes put down in black and white. I would thank my family for tolerating me and treating me better than I deserve every time.

My fate for being that nice to me and making my dream of this book come true. I thank my friends who make life look worthwhile.

And most importantly, someone who made everything possible, Ajay Setia. Yes despite of all clashes, it's been real pleasure writing with him. His presence saved me from the headache of worrying about my nonsensical writing. 'Thanks' is too small a word for my biggest critic and best supporter in one soul. Just wanted to say nothing would have been possible without you around.

Harleen Walia

Prologue

❄ ❄ ❄

There has never been a day much awaited for me than today. Though I had longed for this, but reaching where I stand today has meant leaving an infinite things I owned. I can't help but believe. Heading towards the place I never been before, the past is pulling but I have to look forward to figure out my future. A new life, though it is miles away, awaits.

Though I had never imagined it could ever happen, but amidst of thousands of people at Delhi Airport, I feel missing. Through the glass pane, I see people landing and being welcomed by their families, their loved ones. The sight is fruitful indeed.

But this is not the just place, where people accumulate looking forward to their destinations. Rather, it is where uncountable loved ones are forced to part from each other. Ample of thoughts I brushed away before nostalgia takes over me, and find something to do other than anticipating. Having checked-in my luggage at the carousel,holding nothing much in hand, except the bag which carries the things I can never travel without. And something more important!

I pull out my cherished possession as I lie back waiting on the chair and began to write in it about my day so far.

Airport shopping, a variety of nationalities, reunite smiles, heart-shattering partitions, I have so much to write about, but writing in crowd was never been a pleasant experience for me personally. But done enough spotting every possible variety of the crowd and wandering in the place for reunions and good-byes, I made attempts to portray the cobwebs, my mind is caught in to. With less than three lines I wrote, I gave up the idea and close it down.

Attempts to indulge myself in the surroundings failed another time. There's no way possible for me to spend the delayed hours of my flight staring at foreigners with blue hair, and couples with blushing smiles.

Immersed in the world of thoughts, I lay my eyes on its front cover. As I flip through its pages, the calendar catches my attention, as I find the date- 28th July 2012 encircled and 'Only till' written over it. It is today's date.

But I recollect that it was marked 2 months back. Back then, I had no clue that reaching this date would need me to get through so many ravels.

I have not read it since a long back, and the thought of reading is tempting. It encloses memoirs of the past that I could not let it slip through my fingers. Had always been paranoid about being cheery, I'm sure that the last I want is to feel more nostalgic. Finally, I make up my mind and open up the pages on which I have bared my heart from ages. It transports me not to the moment when the mark was drawn, but to a long way back.

I have left that place years ago, and those people who still occupy a place in my life, a few others, a corner in my heart, that I can never take back. I wonder sometimes if I miss something, Sometimes, I smile back to the question, and sometimes I laugh it out. But most of the time, I tend to ignore it. But the real answer and all that I want to say is:

The First Light

* * *

29th September 2007

"Hello..."

"Where, the hell, have you reached man?" Pulkit asked, as he cuts me off in the rudest tone his vocal cordcapable of producing. Not that it's the way he talk. In fact, it was quite in contrast to his simple peaceful demeanour. He hardly ever lost his calm. But that morning, his voice was pouring furiousness. Something that I had not witnessed since the day we became friends.

I met Pulkit in the 2nd week of the college and in the very first interaction he told me that he was an odd one out in a class of amazing snobs.

"I'm just on the way, dude. Just reached!" I said, trying to pacify his anger.

"That is exactly what you told me half an hour ago. I'm waiting for you like fools from past one hour." I removed the cell-phone from my ear and checked the time, as Pulkit continued to blow curses over me. My goodness, it was already 10 a.m.!!!!

I could hear his presumably high voice as I re-placed the phone. "No matter how fast you ride, we'll need another half an hour to travel down the 28 km-long stretch."

"Calm down, we won't." I said, looking at things messed up around me.

"Just tell me a thing. Are you coming to pick me up or should I find another way to reach my fresher's party?"

"Buddy chill, don't worry. I'm right on the way. I'll pick you up in exactly ten minutes. By the way, it is my fresher's too."

"Alright, no more than that."

"Yeah yeah, but for that I need to abort the call and ride faster. See you. " I said and hung up the phone, not to ride but to change into my clothes.

The very moment Pulkit called, I had just stepped out of the bathroom and was yet to get ready. But, telling him my actual physical location would have meant inviting death.

In a nick of seconds, I wore my favourite white shirt, a pair of denims, and my new jacket which I bought for the occasion. My fastest ever! I struggled with my hair as my mind imagined Pulkit getting mad at meas it was almost 10:25 a.m.

At times, when you beg time to run slower, your clock shoots up like a speedometer racing up and higher. I left home as I saw Pulkit's call again. Before I left, I made sure that I had picked up what I needed the most, the bag.

Pulkit was already standing out his house as I reached there. Putting on the charade of ire, he hardly acknowledged my emergence. But like always he could not help keeping himself off the mark of sarcasm, as he said that ironic 'Thank you'. On my end, I crossed my heart that it was really tough to recognize him at a distance.

Today what made me awestruck was his dressing. In

that black shirt and denims, he looked better than ever. His glasses replaced by contacts, I mean, where was my nerdy best friend? But, he had painted a sore expression on his face. And those expressions could give complex to any pouting kid. Sad for him, they did nothing else than make me laugh. That's all I do, misplacing my laughter to raise other's anguish all the time.

But, I dared not mess it up anymore for the badly disappointed, almost blood thirsty friend of mine. To control my muted laughter, I said, "Looking dashing, bro." But his expression clearly said that he was not in the mood to get entertained. He was infuriated as hell. I was thinking hard to find something to ease his silent grumble and help him improve that grave expression, when finally he uttered something rather than just staring me.

"May we please proceed now, or I suppose you have planned to spend the entire day right here??" He said.

"No no. I'm really very sorry. I'm really."

"There you are. It's ok. Chuck it now." He said. I envy people who can chuck the disturbances so easily. But I'd warned you this is Pulkit. The calm, sensible and forgiving guy, people silently ask for in their prayers.

"Let's go. By the way." I said.

"What does this huge bag carry?? Don't tell me we have to go somewhere else too now."

"We don't. And this is for youuuur fresher's party only." I said, reflecting sarcasm in my voice.

"Oh, and it carries what??"

"A keyboard." I answered, waiting when his queries would end and we would start with the journey.

"Keyboard! What for?? Where is the monitor and processor, Mr. Potential computer engineer??" He said. It seemed like now it was his turn to test my patience.

"Man, this is not the computer's keyboard. It's my

musical keyboard!!!"

A week before the Fresher's Party, our seniors had invited us all. While many of my classmates frightened as if they were man-eaters, I was keen about the interaction.

Nonetheless, I was thoroughly excited by the idea when they announced that aspirants for the Mr. & Ms. Fresher's tag could prepare mono-performances. And for me, playing keyboard was not any option, but the only choice. It was the only thing I remembered I had enjoyed the most till the journey so far.

"Keyboard?? Synthesizer!! Ever heard of a thing like that??"

"Of course, I must have been out of my mind to ask such a thing. But, it will be really difficult for you to hold it and drive. ."

"It will be, but when did I say I'm the one holding it??" I shrugged.

He understood the mischief in my voice. "It means what??"

"Means you. Do hold the keyboard firmly." I smiled at him.

"No way. I'm just not carrying this." "But why??"

"What do you mean by why ??

"I'm just not ruining the crease of my suit for holding this rack-sack of yours."

"Suit? Well placed concerns, Huh?" I said with the hint of irony, as Pulkit rolled his eyes.

"Dude, do you realize I have left Tanya just because I could pick you up?? And you are calling my keyboard a rack-sack."

"You left Tanya?? You??" he was stunned by my last statement.

"Yes, may be if I would have offered her a lift, she would not have denied. But I preferred you over the girl I like. And that's how you pay me back??" I said blushing, and overjoyed in my heart of hearts dreaming something that had rare chances of coming true.

"Ohoho. As if she is dying to on your bike?"

"Who knows she might be??" I said in an optimistic tone which 90 percent of Indian guys survive on. Pulkit almost realized there was hardly any point in rebelling any further. "Fine. Give it to me, you keyboard lover." He sat on the bike as I pressed the clutch and started the bike. "Uhm, music lover precisely." I corrected him.

"Yeah, and get your Tanya to hold this on the way back. I'll travel by a bus." Pulkit said, teasing me.

I smiled wondering how conveniently we guys dragged a chic into our rifts, that too when she is immeasurably far-off in a totally another world. Tanya had become my 'crush', if that word was appropriate for what I felt for her. I still remember the first time I noticed her, while she was struggling with a program in the Computers lab. Not a surprise that she was so engrossed that she did not even notice me, working just next to her, who was engrossed in noticing her. Words like 'cute', 'pretty' seem an understatement for girls like her. Fortunately, we got to talk when I helped her debugging the error from the program.

From that very moment, I could not help looking at her and stealing a glance whenever possible. She was completely worth it. In fact, much more. But after that, there was a rare chance that we could talk. She was always surrounded by her friends. And even when she was not, all I could manage to say was a 'Hii' and run out of her sight. Many a times, her presence in the radius of 2 meters made me nervous and heart pick up its pace.

Fortunately, we were not as late as Pulkit had assumed us to be at Hotel Saffron, known faces with unrecognised gestures welcomed me. So much that I could write about my classmates out there, but in one line- Make-up has the ability to change looks terrifically, and sometimes terribly. In the land of blondes, I was searching for that girl with dark hair whose images had been haunting me since the moment I entered the Party Hall. For Tanya! Magic spread across the hall, as I saw her in that red dress. She looked arresting. The very second my glance fell upon her, my heart went off to her. I would be the happiest man, if only I could tell her that. But even before I could manage to look at her properly, the seniors made a call.

Standing at the stage, I could almost see everyone present there. The beautifully decorated hall sent me sparks of enthusiasm. Bunches of tulip flowers interlaced the party hall of Hotel Saffron. Dim florescent lights, glinting after every couple of seconds, complimented the ambiance making it even perfect. Each one of us was being called up for the 'introduction' round.

Most of the girls were looking pretty. Some of them even drop dead gorgeous. But, no fraction of my imagination could make Tanya look better than she did that day. She was a piece of marvel. My eyes ran across the hall to find my sugared treat. I had seen her only twice from the moment I had come. Unable to spot her, my smile began to fade. But I had to keep up, as the host gave me a green signal to start my introduction.

With words reflecting utmost courtesy to the seniors and my friends, I began my introduction. Eyes surely got widened when I lied a bit about my aggregate in 12th std., giving a boost of certain percents, some due to appreciation of our seniors, while some because of disgust, of those who knew it was a hoax.

I expressed my fondness for music, the only icing on my sponge cake. How did I miss that? I spoke with utter confidence and fluent. Luckily, Google had given me enough catchy words. A number of practices, that I did last night in front of the mirror, bore fruits and I was promoted to the next round.

When the rest of my classmates were choosing what to perform in the performance round, unexpected consciousness was taking all over me. All of a sudden, carrying the keyboard seemed pretty odd over other simple idyllic options like singing or dancing.

It was undoubtedly an extra effort, I knew from the beginning, but I did not want anyone to infer with it as an over-hyped act.

“You look uncomfortable, what is wrong??” Pulkit asked, as we stood in the backstage.

“Nothing, do you think keyboard will look like an exaggerated effort for a mere round?” Even if I try, I could not hide anything from him.

“Are you nuts?? It would not. People are performing. So are you. Nothing’s wrong about that.”

“But it would appear childish or may be a publicity stunt.” I said, recklessly confused.

“As if you don’t need publicity?? Do you know you are over-rating yourself??” He mocked.

“This is not the perfect time to make fun, man.”

“Yeah. Don’t make faces. You are just complicating damn simple things, give your silly mind some peace. Now, pickup your keyboard and go ahead. It’ll go great.” He said.

“Are you saying this because you really feel so or the reason behind is that you don’t want your hard work of carrying the keyboard go waste??” I teased him, as my name was announced.

“To be honest, the latter actually.” He said, as we both laughed.

A keyboard is irresistibly pulling for my fingers, and how much I loved this fact, when I was up there for performing.

I played two songs which expressed the elation and ecstasy of the new college students, which instilled Zeal among the audiences. And seeing them enjoy, my confidence soared up. The reaction that came from their side was even better than my expectations. The round of applause that followed after the 6-minute long performance made it evident to me that bringing a keyboard could not be a mistake. It was surely not. My other classmates had done well at their turns. They were awarded as talented voices or elastic bones.

In the 3rd round, the judgment panel was meant to shoot questions to the finalists for Mr. & Ms. Fresher's tag.

"My question to you is 'What's your take on life?'" The only girl amongst the judges asked me, as I stood with three competitors.

Deep in my heart, I had a blast, the moment she completed her question. Because I felt the answer to her question was as easy as grabbing a candy from a 6year-old. I began thinking of an impressive answer, but almost the next moment, the announcer asked me to start answering.

I glanced at the judges, brought the mike closer and very confidently, I began to speak. "Thank you for the question. I think life, for me, is a thing to……. is a thing to….."

Crash!!!! A thing to do what?? I had no clue what to say next and I had no clue from where did those words that I had uttered come. That's what happens when you start speaking without giving a thought. I felt as if my tongue got tied and I was completely speechless for a couple of moments that followed. One of the judge who sat in front gave a 'c'mon-you-can-do-it' look, gesturing me to try again.

I did, but it proved out to be nothing more than a failing attempt. Once I lost it, I could not get it back. I began to feel embarrassed, and stole eyes from everyone. But, it could not stop them from seeing **me** in my worst situation till then.

However, the three guys sitting in the front were angels

from heaven. No less than that! To rescue me out of the ordeal, they put up another question. "Never mind. So, tell us about your journey in the college so far. What has it been like??"

This time, I was given around 20 seconds to formulate a good answer or at least an answer. "I believe that our college is a wonderful place, and my journey so far has been really good. I. . . I have. ." I suddenly paused in the middle of my statement. Not again please, I prayed. But that was all I managed to speak, when just a moment ago, I had a zillions of things running in my mind, which were good enough to be spoken about.

Silence prevailed for 5 seconds, 6, 7.., 8.... Just as the moments passed, anxiety soared in me, choking me up. I tried hard to recompile my thoughts and to blurt out any sensible thing in English, but it was no cake walk for me. At least not when 200 eyes were staring at me, in the most embarrassing situation, I had been caught till then. I was questioning to my senses, pleading them to reply and ended up cursing them. It seemed as if my brain had gone for hibernation. I felt helpless, useless, paralyzed. I gave up. There was no point in standing there at the stage making others enjoy my frailty any further.

"Yeah it was good, that's it." I said, returned the mike, and stepped down from stage. I was completely pale by then. I had gone numb. My chances of becoming Mr. Fresher were out of the question. I did not even bother about it.

Manav was titled as Mr. Fresher that evening. I barely stood a chance after all that happened. It hardly made any difference to me.

But I hated why on earth, was English brought to my country, why?? And, if it was, then why could not I manage to mumble few lines fluently. Why did it prove out to be so notorious when I least expected it to happen? I wished to forget the throat-thickening nightmare. But on the other end, I wanted to remember it forever, commit it into my memory forever. So, that it could haunt me every now & then and rake me up.

Once you are in college, things seem to be rushing. Time sprints. Events follow another and the series becomes never-ending. Internal exams of my engineering popped up the very next week. Owing to my competitive nature, I gulped down every subject's course and performed quite well.

The internal practicals occupied us with bundles of files and papers. And, the semester exams began in no time. The six subjects our first semester offered could not be called tough by any measure. They were not, at least not for species that had born to burn the endless torturing syllabus of physics, chemistry and Maths for the past two years of their lives.

Our subjects were in fact very engrossing and pulled me harder to gen up more. By God's grace and my preceding guy's assistance, the exams went off well. The end of external practicals and viva-voca concluded the first semester, on January 10th, 2008.

The college re-opened in the first week of February. I was fresh yet strong headed to start up with the second semester. Almost a month at home, though I missed college a bit, but life is a thing filled with joy, and peace. The days passed lying on the bed while the nights, chatting with random people over social networking sites. I had shown my face to all my kith and kin who had declared my existence as endangered, because of my schedule during the high school. However, I had utilized my vacations in one real good sense. I had set my mind and decided the direction of the boat I wanted to sail in. I had prepared myself for the upcoming semester & the syllabus to mug up was awaiting me. 'Proper attention to knowledge' was the second semester's resolution. Learn the world beyond books.

I was clear about my aim. I wanted to do well at everything, especially in academics. It is something everybody longs for, whenever a new semester commences.

Exactly from February, I became damn sincere. I attended almost all the lectures and more importantly, listened carefully to everything being taught. I utilized the free time in the internet lab.

I could not believe Pulkit calling me nerdy, until that one day. I was taken by surprise when Tanya came up to me and asked me for the solution of a numerical. Some of her friends were entitled geeks from day one of college. So, she really did not have to ask me. After all, geeky was their trademark.

To the weirdest of my luck, initially I fumbled by her charisma. Tanya walking to ask me for something in a class of over 60 was surreal. I mean, even if it was for a stupid question, she really thought I could do better than others. The mere thought was enough to amuse me, and take me on cloud nine. And all I did was flipping through pages of her notebook, and stealing sights at safe intervals. If only someone could tell her what the reason behind confusion of my mind was. It was her! But, when she said, "I thought you might know how to crack this." I tried again and succeeded.

Pulkit, sitting next to me, was apparent only after Tanya left. It would not be a lie if I state that a hundred people could go unnoticed when she stood 2 inches away from me. Pulkit winked at me, as I tried to change the topic.

"Have you tried the derivations given to us?"

"Uhm, no, I thought you must know how to crack them." He said imitating Tanya's tone. And added sheepishly, "Mr. Certified Nerd."

The month of March had unexpected things in store. Things I had never guessed. Like we already heard, the annual college fest was to be organized in the end of March or in the first week of April. So, the preparations for it had taken a start. The techno- cultural fest meant lots of zeal, fun and the best part, abundance of free lectures. Rest of the college was preparing plays, choreographing dance performances, singing songs, making robots, designing applications, and what not.

My friends and I were enjoying the time of our life. Anybody rarely attended classes and so did we. Escaping out of the class had become our daily routine, by giving a believable excuse to the professors. The objective meant sitting in the cafeteria or corridors, playing and watching the commotion around us.

We were sitting in the cafeteria, forming a group when Raman, a senior called me. He was one of the guys involved in our fresher's party. He gestured me to come out of the group. I did as he asked me to do, making an excuse from my friends.

"Hey." He said, as we shook hands. "Hi. How were you, Sir??"

"I'm doing fine. Did not see you after the party?? The star's too busy, I guess." He made a dig at me.

"Don't embarrass me, Sir. I was just occupied with exams." "Yeah, I see. People do study a lot in the first year, a lot." I nodded. "And after that??"

He laughed at my question as I felt that I had ridiculed him. "You'll know it by yourself, man. So, what's up?? Must be performing at the fest??" gave him a "does-my-face-look-like-I-can" look. "Uhm, notreally." I said and thought of the possible things I could do to entertain the mass. My technical skills were not even in their infancy. I was a singer by no chance, and taking my dancing abilities into consideration, accepting me could not be called as a real grace for any dancing group. And acting would be such a nightmare for the viewers.

"Tell me, would you like to perform??" "As in??"

"I mean playing keyboard. Do you know we have a "battle of bands' competition too??"

I thought for a couple of seconds & then answered, "Yeah, I have heard, a bit though." Of course, I had not, but I was in no state to say 'no' to that. Especially, after the kind of expression that he wore, I did not want to let him down and consider me ignorant either.

"Good. Look, many bands have proved their mettle on the performance ground, & I tell you, it's a great opportunity." He said things that were too convoluted for me to grasp. "Aryan, let's make it easier. I can recommend you to a band, if you want."

"Really?? Is it possible??"

"Hmmm. Everything is. And you must, must go for it." He sounded really convincing. "And you'll learn a lot with them, if things go smooth."

"Sure if you say so. Then I would like you to talk to them. Go ahead, Sir."

"Wonderful..!"

Two days later, I was informed by Raman that a music band called "VISHESH" wanted to listen to my keyboard.

"You know that these guys are mostly coming from the second year itself." Raman said, as we climbed up the staircase to make our way to the practice room.

"Ohh?? So, all of them??"

"Yes, except the guitarist who is from the final year. But they are really good guys, adjustable people. If you get selected, you'll have long way to go." He said, while I was trying to keep composed and not to worry.

"Sir, is there any requirement in their band?? I mean, for a keyboard player??"

"Not actually, but they have promised me that they can accommodate a keyboard player, if they find you to be up to the mark." He said, pointing me to the room. I nodded. I played two songs of my choice, just like they had asked me to. And to be honest, they were much different from what I had expected them to be. No arrogance, no superiority.

After spending half an hour with them, I could remark that there was a sense of stability had made home in those guys, something that I lacked, that most of the people I have known before lacked. However, in no sense, it could be inferred as they were dull. They made fun of each other, pulled my legs too, and played music for joy, their real joy.

After my turn, they played a song together, quite enjoyable. I had not heard that song before, but they had surely made good music. They asked me, if I could try playing that song too. But, I told them honestly that it was the first time I had heard that it.

Like I thought without making any complaints, they were sweet enough to play it again for me and even help me along the performance. After a few trials, I was able to catch up the rhythm and I succeeded in playing the first snippet of the song. I was enjoying it.

"That sounds impressive, man." Their lead singer said, after I could play the song without much assistance. I was happy to get appreciated. Who isn't?

"It is. So, from when have been you playing the keyboard?" Their drummer asked me.

"Some five to six years, Sir. As far as I can remember from standard eighth!"

He smiled and said, "Very good. It shows you had." "Aryan, we do consider you're really skilled, but…." One of them spoke and shook his head.

I raised my eyebrows, waiting him to complete and wondering what that shaking of head meant. Why do people take pauses and kill other's with suspense when they are not ought to do that? I finally asked, "But??"

"Do you have another keyboard?? Larger than this one??" "No, this is the only one I possess right now."

"Actually, none of us doubt your potential,in fact, we have rarely ever seen someone playing that good in his first year. But, what bothers us is that your keyboard is somewhat smaller than a stage performance's requirement."

"Ohhh!! So, this one won't work." I was disappointed.

"If it would, then we would have been happier. But unfortunately, it won't. Can you get a new one?? Or arrange it from somebody ??"

I thought for a while. "I don't know, Sir. I need to think on this regard. But, I have performed on this SA-21 many a time."

"Of course, but there's a lot difference between an individual performance and a band performance, isn't it? See, if you are able to get it, it'll surely help you in future too."

One of the guitarists said, trying to convince me.

"You're right." I nodded. "Sir, I'll surely try. I'll make up my mind, and inform you."

"Sure."

After I left their room, I thought what might be happening inside. May be I should get another or not. Dad would definitely say 'no',even if I push him even a lil.

So, the decision relied upon me.

Yes, no doubt they were good musicians, but a larger keyboard would cost around Rs. 20000. May be even more than that. Does a mere stage performance in college worth that amount, I wondered. Plus, I would have to practice along with them throughout the day, missing out all fun that the rest of my classmates would have. And, still it might not end up anywhere. I may not be able to match up with their work.

I was nowhere willing to buy a new keyboard. To say the least, I chuck out the thought that I was offered by a band called 'VISHESH'.

We were free and untamed as birds in those days. And, the study-hard-and-alike promises I had made at the beginning of the semester got buried in their graves unannounced. But there was something which really bothered the hell out of me. Tanya had been a part of her group, quite from the first month of the college, but now there was something unusual when she sat with them. Noticeable indeed!

Most of the times, she was with Manav. Always with him. And even while they were in a group, a few sparks could be seen flying between the two of them. I often pondered what I felt when I saw them together. Some sort of creepy feeling that flared up my interiors! I wanted to tell her something, may be to stay away. But then, who was I to tell that. It was her life, I guess.

I never guessed before!!

* * *

The much awaited annual fest began on the eve of29th march. We were all really excited as it was the first annual fest of our engineering life. The college was decorated beautifully with pools of lights all around made our spirits soar. The stage's backdrop was completed by the largest possible and the most beautiful canvas anyone had ever witnessed in their lives, making it mark as heart of the college.

Feeling of happiness, pride, ecstasy, with pangs of expectations rising higher every second. The atmosphere was never better before. The performances began at 11:30 a.m. other colleges were too part of the performances, making it a grand show and provide a neck-to-neck competition.

They all exhibited their remarkable talent, making the first day flawless. And, the war among competitiors, the art and the audiences always made it a win-win. We got to see ultimate breathtaking performances.

On the second day,we had dramatic skits and the musical performances. 'Battle of bands' was one of them. So far I heard, four bands from other colleges, and two from ours were going to participate. I had heard a lot about one, the final year band. Also, a newly called 'VISHESH'

Was joining that year. Quite unknowingly, I had a deep desire to watch that band's performance. I wanted to see how these guys performed.

Occasionally, the 'battle of bands' began with G.N.C.T's band at 6:30 p.m. It was the first time, I was watching a band performing live in front of my eyes. And watching meant believing! To my surprise, a band performance was much more than I thought. Every passing second made me feel curious about what was to come next.

After G.N.C.T and E.L. College's performance, 'VISHESH' came to light.

VISHESH's performance began with the twelve minuteslongsound check, after which they performed their first song.

The appreciation they got from the audiences put the first two performances into shade. The crowd went even crazier, as they kicked off further. The supreme performance made the audiences roar and roar. It was really that good. I could see them all, their faces glowing. That moment made them resemble stars. Real stars, who could make others mad for themselves; who were capable enough to make others die to swap positions with them. I so wanted to be one of them, performing at the stage. That was when I realized the blunder I committed in my sheer ignorance. I must have gone berserk to say no to VISHESH.

I could have been one of them, and I got the chance so easily. But call it my childishness or stupidity, I slapped the opportunity in its face. Even Pulkit understood that. His one statement was enough to make me feel guilt. He said,"-Look at them. You would have surely lost it, man, when you denied them."

How could I be so oblivious to their potential?

While VISHESH performed, everybody could see them, so could I. But, there was a gap between me and band that could never be bridged. For them I was another face in the crowd, an unrecognised, unfamiliar face. And, I was responsible for that to happen. At last, my heart answer, Yes, a performance like that was worth the price of a new keyboard. It was not a 'mere' performance. I wished I could go back and stop myself from declining the golden chance, but life is not that easy, I guess. It was too late to regret, too late to ponder.

After 'VISHESH' stepped down, the final year's band 'Zenith' came to perform. And if VISHESH was magic,they were supernatural. A hundred words of praise for them could be justified. In fact, they deserved more. Their performance set the stage on fire. They were the epitome of stardom, of celebrations, of life.

Fate had taught me a lesson that night, which I could never fail to forget. That night, when VISHESH's impac made the world fall at their feet, I sat in darkness till 2 A.M. replaying VISHESH's performance in my mind over and again, and waiting for dear slumber to bring me some peace. But, I hardly fell asleep, finally made a commitment to my promise.

Life after the fest rolled on to the way it was in the month of February. I wanted something to focus on. And what could be better than internal exams during then.. I worked harder, and scored well.

Even apart from the internal practicals, I tried to stay on my toes, making myself aware. At college, rest of the things occupied us. From mid-may itself, our preparatory leaves or the popularly called P.L.s began. However, the name I feel is a misnomer for most of the engineering students in our country. For us, calling them as 'semi-vacations' would be more appropriate. During the P.L.s, my schedule was much familiar to the one I had in my winter break after the first semester exams, except for one necessary change. The long night chats were replaced by long night gen ups. After all, studying was the need of the hour.

My result for the first semester was out and I had scored 75.8%, ranked number four in my class. It was something that I did not like. Perhaps, it pushed me to gulp more and more chapters. With all my preparations, I waited for the last exams of first year. As per the convention, after the final practical, the second semester of my engineering got winded up by the end of June.

Another beautiful phase of our lives awaited as almost two months long stretched vacations got winded up. The second year of our college life, of our engineering, had taken a start. I was very keen to look forward to it.

No longer we were called as 'freshers'. We were now the seniors.

There's one thing about growing up in college life. A distinct feeling of pride comes along with getting older. Or at least, we felt something cool about it. No more chances of giving introductions in cafeterias, no more alienated looks, no more references just-out-**of**-school-kids.

Nevertheless, now we were the one making fun of the first year guys in every possible manner. This is a universal fact. Everybody, no matter how nerdy or how spoilt they are at their time, love doing deep analysis on the childishness spread over their juniors, for at least once.

The day, fourth of October, 2008, my much awaited birthday. I was keenly for an opportunity to ask for a keyboard as my birthday present from mom and dad. I had reasoned well that the keyboard I possessed from three years had become too small for me. But, the moment when I told them about the offer , it did wonders for me. A Yamaha-410 keyboard was mine on the very next day.

The excitement for my newly-owned present's obsession magnetized me towards home early before time, bunking the last lectures almost for a week to play the keyboard, which had burnt a tiny-miny hole of Rs. 17,650 in dad's pocket.

Not just the excitement but the gusto escalated, as the years progressed. The group-ism in our class touched the sky and so did the flame wars. It was during lunch when we began to have our meals when four of our classmates went to the dais. Manav, Ankit, Tanya and Rohit.

Before anyone of us could figure out what their motive was, Manav announced, "Guys, we have a news to announce. We all are well aware that he have to host a fresher's party, as we are seniors now. So, we have decided to make it happening on 22nd October, 11:00 a.m. The venue is hotelMadrid." He said that in one breathe.

He being titled as 'Mr. Freshers' made made really no difference to me, but every glance of that guy after he turned to be Tanya's closest friend tortured me. The 'Tanya' thing was really thorny.

"Guys, the juniors have given a really nice feedback and are equally thrilled. Those who want to come and join us...... "

"When did they manage to plan all this??" Pulkit asked me, as they continued to rant about 'their' plan.

"I'm equally clueless." I said to him.

"And what is she doing behind him?" Pulkit uttered, looking at Tanya, as if she asked for my exclusive permission to walk up there. I made a face and just shrugged.

"Please deposit the money before 14th if you are interested, so that we can make the advance payments for the arangements" Manav's confident tone was so sky-rocketed as if the director of the college had especially walked up to him and requested him to host the fresher's party. Then, he added as an afterthought,

"Any queries?"

Nobody answered back. It seemed as if they had turned

into statues. "Guys, you can ask if you have any kind of queries, please." The same silence yet again prevailed. Were they deaf? I could not afford to let him go and become a hero, was what I knew. At least, not this time.

He said, "Alright then. So, I'd take it as all clear. Tha..n…k… "

"I have a query." I said, stopping him in the middle of his statement, as I got up from my seat.

"Go ahead." He said with a nod.

"Tell me, do we all appear as fools out here??" I asked, in a no-nonsense tone, taking wind out of "Hero of the day",Mr. Manav. His disciples who stood behind him on the dais were equally stunned, Tanya the most observable among them.

"What?? What do you mean by that**??"**He said.

"Oh, if I am not very clear, let me elaborate, dear. Do we look like fools who are just here to get invited for the same fresher's party for which every one of us is equally responsible, but you took the charge."

"Excuse me, Aryan. Someone had to. But why do you think you people are not involved**?"**

"Because we are not. And it's because a few snobs think that we are not capable of managing it."

"Oh really?? So that's what you think. Huh??"

"Whatever. But, I assume that there's hardly one person who has perceived the idea that way. They don't have any problem. Do they??" He said, looking towards the rest of the class.

Oh God, this jerk should try in politics. Engineering is such a waste of his time, I wondered.

"Ok. Then let's find out. Guys, all those who are keen and supportive about the freshers' eve arranged by our very dear friends, please, raise your hands." I announced, sarcasm in my voice reflected. Three of my classmates raised their hands.

"And now, those who are not in favor and would want

things to take a turn, please raise your hands." I had made an rough estimation of what was going to come out, before I spoke that statement. I had crossed my fingers.

Around 13 or 14 hands came up. The rest of our classmates looked like they hardly had any interest in the world around them. The number was quite less than the expected, but thank God, we still led in the ratio.

"It's clear." I smirked towards Manav. His complexion turned almost red. What a snapshot moment it was!

And then, Tanya finally took the charge, "Look guys, it's evident that you people are hurt, but we had no such intentions. Aryan, you have really interpreted it wrong." A chill ran down my spine as she mentioned my name. I tried to keep my expression as calm as I could. In less than a moment, the anger, furiousness went missing.

Say something, goddamit, my senses told me. But what could I say to her?? Even though she was supporting an arrogant swine, scolding a girl who has such acute eyes was not my cup of tea. And the cuteness augmented every time they got widened. I tried to suppress my blushing smile, and find some words to save myself from Pulkit's upcoming scoffs.

Before I could manage to say anything, one of our Classmate spoke, "No Tanya, Aryan's right. We have an equal say. It's matter of our entire class. "And we can't be denied from that." They were all finally taking a stand for themselves.

"But….." She tried to defend, but hardly found any words. Even Manav fell short of words. His heroism, his over-confidence had evaporated.

"But, yes, if someone tries to disapprove, we can make sure that the juniors take off their hands from any bullshit. They would prefer turning down 4 seniors rather than going against the rest majority." I said.

He said, "Guys, try and understand. We have committed and planned everything. You can't ruin them."

"We couldn't only if you had bothered asking us before doing that. But sad to say, your plans had a short life."

"But you guys are welcomed to get involved, even in organizing team." He said. What was that now, compensation or compromise! Nobody reacted to that. Our silence was a tight slap at their faces, at their egos. It must have been harder for Manav, the mastermind. Ahh!

After a couple of minutes, Manav finally uttered, "That's it. Do what you want, guys. You can organize the party all by yourself. None of us will intervene." Not only us, but his friends too were shocked for wht he said. .

"Are you sure??" I asked thoroughly enjoying the spicy moment.

"Damn sure! Note my words. We'll meet you at the fresher's." He said. His friends would have wanted to murder him for promising that. But it was too late.

"In that case, thank you so much."

We were all content. We were merry because we had restored our right to organize the fresher's party. But I was happy because I had given it back to that weird smug. I had finally brought him down, when he was on a trip of his own.

At our turn to organize the fresher's party, we tried and involved everyone who was interested. We discussed and then decided, whether it was the date, the venue, timings, theme, or the events. I made sure that nobody gets any chance to point out fingers at us. In a duration of just 3 days, we were able to put everything in place and make the occasion a real success. Even though Manav arrived the party , his grave expressions clearly explained how forced his presence was. Watching the entire charge in our hands, he got irritated even more. And there she was, Ms. Tanya supporting her best friend. She did not leave his side, not even for once. If only I could know, why did she have to do everything I hate!

My college life became quite different than I imagined. In the beginning I promised to study like nerd but my mind floated elsewhere. But I was not the one to be blamed for getting diverted when a girl like Tanya is around.

When I was in college, I kept stealing glances at her and when I return, her thoughts kept me occupied. No wonder I was lost in thoughts of the girl who was nowhere near me. I could never gather enough courage to walk up to her in person and talk. However, my kind destiny did give me an offer to break ice on a fine day. Diwali was around the corner which ignited a lot of exciting things, the best among was the college's Diwali party. We were celebrating the occasion that epitomized light and happiness in life. Students of all the departments were asked to bring clay lamp to the building of their respective departments.

"Look at them, they are so excited as if they have been invited to participate in Miss India pageant." I told Pukit as we laughed at the girls of my class. The moment this news reached our classroom, some of the girls started making plans about how to formulate the decorating team and make our block look the best. Rajat, one of my classmate started asking for the volunteers who wanted to be in the decorating team, I wondered how a guy could be as artistic as he was. Honestly, Rajat's painting and drawing skills had been a hot topic of discussion among girls since day one.

Point to be noted, there are two kind of boys who exist on earth, great painters and others who are no where familiar with the word 'painting'. I was specifically in the latter category. Not that I had tried painting much, I was too occupied with music in my life to try art and craft. So decorating was a big 'No' as I saw my classmates volunteering for being a part of the team.

"Yeah right, decoration team, ehh? Not just excited, they are damn serious about it. "

"Like it is a JEE or AIEEE." I chuckled and asked Pulkit

"Why don't you join them? Even you are not bad at this stuff."

"And you imply that I am not that good. Is that so?" It does. C'mon, we both know painting is your thing.

What else do you do after returning home except those alpha and beta? Why don't you go for it?" I budged him as he nodded.

"Chuck it. I would have volunteered but I have to leave for

Delhi tomorrow morning you know well. So I better out of it, some other time may be." Pulkit said. More than painting, procrastination was his thing. And even if he had not been going, nobody could push him. "But you will volunteer for this." He said interrupting my thoughts.

"Why would I? I have no reason to do so." I said, as he looked at Tanya and winked back at me. Before I could say a word, I saw Tanya joining the team as volunteer. She smiled at her best, and suggested so many things in just one moment.

"I think we could definitely decorate the department with charts, lights and colorful ribbons. But everybody will do the same, right. What we can do better is make a huge chandelier outside the block. Or winds chime. Inside the block we can use signboards made by us that could help the visitors guide to the place they want to visit. And we can make a WEB inside the block that will be made of…uhm…" Tanya stopped to think. If she looked sweet, her voice was a miracle. As she went on to express her ideas, she had no idea how mesmerized a guy was who stood ten meters away from her. When she told the class about her creative ideas, her smile looked cuter, her eyes looked bigger. A million things had been running in her mind to beautify the block, but in my mind only one thing was running, just to be with her. Within a minute or two, I told Rajat that I would like to join the decorating team as well. As Rajat was amazed by his friend's all-of-a-sudden interest, Pulkit was smirking at me.

That I guess is the difference between friends and best friends. They know you better than you know yourself.

The team comprised of 4 boys and thrice that number girls, was ready to lay down a strategy, I day dreamed about my prospective interaction with Tanya who continued to impress me while detailing her ideas. It would not be wrong to say that she was leading us.

"So, the plan is almost ready. And we'll proudly go with the idea of chandelier, the charts, the caricatures, the puppets.

That would be great for now." Rajat said.

"Plus, we will use the lights as high as we can." One of my classmates suggested.

"We will for sure." Tanya said.

"But guys, important of all we should keep all this a secret, and make sure the unique ideas doesn't get leaked to the other departments." I said.

"Aryan is absolutely correct, guys. We must ensure this till the end." Tanya said. I smiled back at her as she continued, "and we should start up with the plan as soon as possible."

"Yes, we should bring all the things we will need." We had decided to make best use of the things we use every day like we could use CD's for making winds chime, I suggested at the risk of making a fool of myself. But luckily it worked. In fact, Tanya loved it. Though I had never noticed before but many others were also good at creativity. Finally, it was decided that Tanya and two of her friends will go to the market to get all the material required.

Usually when Tanya was around me, I felt stuck for no reason. I could hardly utter a word in front of her, I always hated it. But that day I did not know what boosted me, my confidence was stable, that made me behave like I usually did.

"Guys, may I help? I have a bike, so you don't have to walk such a long stretch." I suggested them.

"I think we must consider Aryan's suggestion. But

that won't be a problem?" Rajat asked me.

"Of course not buddy. In fact, I would love to help. But somebody have to come with me since I know very less about the material." I said.

"Yes, somebody will come with you. Let's see who."

Tanya said.

"A girl Who knows these things better" I said.

"Andit's Tanya". One of Tanya's friends suggested. I was flabbergasted at the suggestion.

"Exactly. Tanya should go." Others said, considering her knowledge about art and craft.

As Tanya willing agreed to come, I was on cloud nine. Tanya and I!! Was this for real? Somebody above seemed pleased with me, I knew.

As she double checked with the list of things, we made way out of the classroom.

"Aryan." she said, making my heart pump faster. "Aryan,

Will you be comfortable, you being really helpful I mean I coming with you won't create a problem, right?" She asked.

"Problem…" I said, with a hint of naughtiness.

"Do you mean there's a problem?" The angel standing in front of my eyes grew tensed. 'Cute' I guess was a word made for her. As I kept mum, she budged me for not speaking up. "You can tell me what is running in your mind." To hell, I was looking at her cute locks and deep eyes. I dared not to tell her all that was running in my mind was she herself.

Beautiful girls like her never give appropriate time to guys who are already overwhelmed by their presence to think, and that is why we get certified as nerds.

"No, no problem." I told her. "Tanya, may I ask you something if you don't mind?"

"You may." My highness said, as we almost reached the parking corner.

"You really like drawing and painting, right?"

"Like? LOVE! I just love drawing and painting." As Tanya said this, her eyes twinkled. "You know Aryan, I don't even remember the first time I painted. I was that young.

So you can imagine how much I am fascinated to it."

"You bet I can." I winked. May be painting was to Tanya as what music meant to me.

As Tanya sat pillion on my bike, my smile got widened and my heart could not stop thanking God for a second. Though the stretch was like three kilometers long but I drove as slow as I could. As Tanya's soft hands struggled to hold her huge bag while sitting on the bike, I over took the opportunity and told her, "you can hold the bike, or you can hold me if you are comfortable. It would be ok." I really did not know from where the courage came in me.

She did "Hmmm" and I felt something on my shoulders. It was her right hand. Was this a dream?

As we rode towards the market, I could not stop praying that nobody from home catches me, while I waswandering with the girl on the roads, I had dreamt of. I was so happy that day, but I dreaded my happiness to get lost. As one half of my mind was hoping not to get caught with Tanya, the other half was busy making castles of air about Tanya. I liked her from almost a year now, but today what I felt for her was different.

Undoubtedly, she was the sweetest girl I had met. In fact, she had every quality to become a prized possession for any guy. She was cute, sweet, she was competent in academics. She was enthusiastic (about painting) as I had seen that day before.

I could not stop smiling when she spoke to me, not even for a second. I could not remember the last time I smiled that long.

Even the girl herself said it, "Aryan, I think you too will enjoy this, your smile speak volume. Though, I never thought you'll take interest in art and craft." So that means she thought about me!

"Really? Is that really so?" I asked Tanya who just nodded. "Well honestly, I have never been the painter kind, but I had it on my 'To-do-in-life" list."

"Quite impressive". I am sure you'll end up being smitten by art." said the girl who had smitten me, unknowingly as we walked inside the arts and craft stores.

The moment we walked in, I checked for any acquaintances and thanked God instantly. The shop was mostly occupied with girls, and young mothers collecting things for their toddler's Holidays Homework.

As Tanya entered the shop, all the heads turned towards her and a few towards me. Even, girls stared at her as she walked confidently. I pondered if she knew that she was indeed the perfect combination of cuteness and confidence.

"Uncle, can we get these things, three boxes of Camelin painting colors, Oil Pastels, Paint Brushes."

"Madam, let me get these first." The shopkeeper said, interrupting Tanya and signaled his minion to bring these things.

Tanya checked if she was given the things properly.

"We need stencils, sketching kits, tip markers, charts. Twenty charts would be enough right?" She asked me, raising her eyebrows. How could I say 'no' to her?

"They would be." I replied as I saw the shopkeeper staring at us.

"All right, twenty charts and spray dye kits, sand paints, palate colors, prinking shears for cutting, yes?" As Tanya uttered these words, she resembled an art and craft dictionary. I was stunned as she asked for things that I had never heard of before. Finally Tanya's demands stopped as she got what she called 'bead mosaics'. Meanwhile, I was terrified hearing such difficult names.

As I paid the bill with the money provided by the department, we exchanged numbers and collected the things. We reached back to the college, I felt relieved that nobody saw me with Tanya in the market.

Our team worked on their toes to decorate our department's building, I found a different zeal in Tanya. A zeal which I had not seen in her before and her fondness for painting was completely visible when she drew anything. It was enough to astonish a guy whose arts was restricted to a hut and a river in all the drawing classes. But it was Rajat's courtesy that helped me find some respectable work in the team. I made a very huge collage. Honestly going by my standards, it was tough to believe that I had made it. In the nutshell, I contributed only in the non-artistic things, such as writing slogans and captions. While I was busy in writing caption and she struggling with her paint brush, she mentioned "it would have been fun if Manav would be able to join us?

I could see disappointment on her face. And this Manav word was enough to burn my interiors. I turned my red face to look for marker, silence prevailed for a moment. And I managed to say "where is he?"

"Actually his cousin is getting married, so he will come after Diwali", she said with disappointed face.

"Oh", I said and excused myself within a second where million things ran through my mind. "May be she is missing him", I said to myself, "but this is the time I can utilize and take over, and throw away this Manav thing from Tanya's mind".

I loved working with Tanya,With Tanya's help, we made a wind chime. Precisely she made it, and all I did was finding the material and gluing them together. My life stood still the very moment when Rajat suggested taking a picture of two of us as I tied the wind chime made by us. Even though I just looked okay, that, I guess, that was my best picture ever.

In fact, I still have that picture.

Everybody smiled as the much awaited moment, the Diwali party was a few moments away, but I was not happy. The next morning she would go back home, and I may not get any opportunity to spend time with her again. These thoughts faded my smile. For one second, I was charmed by her as she looked ravishing in her white dress, but another second, I hated her for looking so good, since that would make me miss her even harder. I wonder if it was a sign from god or just a coincidence that we were wearing the same color.

I teased her saying, "C'mon Tanya, stop following whatever I do. You have even worn my color."

"I'm so sorry, but I could not resist following you Aryan." She laughed and added, "Actually it is a tribute to you for being so nice. I did not expect you to be."

"Well their strikes a saying in my mind", "And that is..."

"Never judge a book by its cover."

"Indeed and you know what." Just as she was saying those words, she was called by a professor. Needless to say, I was irked by her absence. Then we were occupied by our classmates. As she spoke to her friends about how we had adorned the block, I wondered if I could ask her if she could return back from home sooner. Perhaps, a 'miss you' won't give her any wrong signals. God knows she might be feeling the same way towards me I thought. Mad I was. Desperations, oh God. But I kept mum and dared not spoil my friendship with her. Finally the efforts by our team paid off as our department was given the Best Decoration Award. My award however was going away from her, the next morning I knew.

The end of October bought a pleasant breeze,s when the winter is in its advent. And laziness too! Pulkit and I was climbing up the staircase to reach our classroom in the 2nd lecture.

"Do you know about the 'talent hunt'??" he said. Our

class room was in the third floor and still two floors away.

"Yeah, I do. I won the title 'people with the craziest best friend' award there??" I mocked.

"Oho. Well-deserved. Congratulations, you jerk."
"Thank you, dear. But which talent hunt??"

"That's what I call sheer ignorance." He said.

"Yeah, do you realize I had not attended college from past two days??" I said in support of my sheer ignorance.

"Despite that you have full detailed information about your girl. From what she ate in those two days to with whom she ate" He said. I thought if I was granted one murder, I would not need much time to decide. It has to be him.

"Whatever. I'm not a stalker. Why would I care what she's up to? I'm least interested now."

"Really? Nice attempt to fool the guy who stays with you throughout the day. Then, why do you steal eyes from her?"

"I don't, and if I do, it's probably because I don't want her to have any misconceptions." I said as a matter-of-fact.

"Whatever. OK, let's come out of it. Actually, it's College's Talent Hunt. They are organizing it from this year. Music, dance, oratory and stuff like that."

"Really?? And why aren't we participating in something??"

"Because it's only for 1st year people. Not for seniors."

"Oh I see. But it'll be good fun. It should have clicked them a year ago."

"Yeah, I wished that too. But we can watch it at least." He said, as I pondered over something else, much more important.

"You want to say something??" He asked me, as I nodded.

He raised his eyebrows to enquire what was on my mind, as I said, "Uhm. We will for sure."

The talent hunt was held on 7th November, and I really

felt something good came out of it apart from just fun. There were many engrossing events but the event that pulled me the most was that a band's performance. VISHESH's!

Even when one of their member had left the college, the four managed to make it a success. Their performance had been a feast to ears, but what thrilled me the most was a ray of hope for me. I could still give it a try. I could be easily accommodated in the band considering their requirements.

Kunal was not just VISHESH's lead vocalist but an acquaintance through Raman. He was aware of my musical capabilities. I approached him and informed him that I had managed to get new keyboard. It was the step for me to go ahead with them, when he said, "Why don't you join us, the coming weekend? We guys practice here."

I reached college exactly at 11 a.m. upon Kunal's instructions. Since it was a weekend, the campus looked deserted except for the hostel-residing species who were wandering around motiveless. Besides, only the love-birds were spotted sitting hand-in-hand all over the place. Interestingly, the love birds even outnumbered the hostlers. I felt unusually nice about being there. A corner of my heart fancied me sitting with Tanya. But my spoilsport mind brought me back to ruthless reality, and I prayed not to see her sitting here with Manav.

On reaching the practice room, I exchanged the pleasantries with everyone. I was comfortable with them now unlike the first time, I was shivering a bit. Tushar among them came up and shook hands with me and questioned, "Remember Tushar, no??"

"Of course, Sir. I'm Aryan." I said, as he nodded. Tushar introduced me to Sandy and Vishal then rest of his band. Just as the conversation proceeded, my nervousness fled away, comforting me.

"Hmmm. So, Kunal told that you bought a new keyboard." Tushar said as we all settled down.

"That's true. I got it a month back." I said,and opened my bag when they asked me to.

I was delighted when they said approvingly, "This can really work wonders for us."

I played a song on my new keyboard, as Kunal directed me, contenting them about my ease with the new keyboard.

I very well knew that one of their member has completed his engineering, I asked Tushar, "Sir, if I'm not wrong, there were five people in your band last year, right?"There was definitely some sort of space in 'VISHESH', Raman told me.

"Yes Aryan, one of our band-mate left and 'VISHESH' needs a new bass guitarist." Tushar informed.

Lead guitarist, yes. Rhythm guitarist, yes. But I had never heard of a bass guitarist till then, but how do I reveal that to them. The last I wanted was to make an impression of a naive frog that has never looked out of his small well. My wicked mind suggested me to beat around the bush. But, a bad impression would not be as harmful as a false one, at least here. I shunned off all the nasty ideas and gathered **cou**rage to inform Tushar, "I'm afraid, I don't really know what makes a bass guitar different from the normal guitar.

Honestly, today is the first time I have heard of it."

"Never mind." He smiled and then played something with the upper strings of the guitar he was holding.

"I think I can play this through my keyboard." I said, after listening carefully.

"Keyboard?? Are you sure??" Tushar asked me.

"I suppose, just give me some time." I said, promisingly.

After searching through the guide provided with the keyboard, I found the bass category with a couple of bass options like sine bass, guitar bass, etc. I played them one by one. Finally, out of all the options, the sine bass matched it up the best. After few minutes, I played the similar sound.

As I finished the note, all three of them looked pleased, Kunal, more than anyone else. It was written all over his face.

"Sounds really good. What do you have to say??" Tushar said, as I finished.

"Truly convincing. We can consider it." Sandy said.

They discussed with each other and finally gave me a green signal and a world of happiness. I was welcomed with open arms by them.

Once while practicing on a weekend, Tushar asked me "Aryan, may I ask what made you drop the idea of performing last year?? I mean you can answer if you don't mind. Nothing hard and fast."

"No, it's OK. I think I was too ignorant back then. And my ignorance made me commit a huge mistake unknowingly. I lost that opportunity, but when I saw you people again in the talent hunt, all my regrets seemed to get vanished." I said. I could see all of them smiling. "You have a great potential, dude. There is hardly any doubt about that." Sandy said.

"True, buddy. We have to walk together for long, I hope." Tushar said, as he smiled.

"So do I, Sir." I said.

In a nick of time, I became even comfortable with them. I became a part of 'VISHESH'. Not just that, we played music together, we ate together, laughed together. Music had created an invisible bond between us, piling us together.

When you are in the semester system, time flies. Our result for the second semester was out, and I had succeeded getting an aggregate of 77%. Meanwhile our semester exams soon approached. And we shifted the weight of our preference to studies for few days. The **rest** of my band-mates were equally competitive and conscious about their studies.

I never wanted music to turn as a distraction in my academics. None of us did. So, we halted the practice and pulled up our socks, this time to study. I studied hard and did well on my part. The third semester got over. But my craving for real music had taken its start.

The morning of 26th February brought us back under the roof of our second home, J.M.I.T. The college welcomed us for the fourth semester. Being accepted as a part of VISHESH, my spirits were high. This semester was going to be more than usual, I registered that in mind on day onebutit offered a jackpot, the annual fest.

It took around ten days for all five of us to get united and hit the practice ground, as the rest of my mates were a year senior to me. Their devotion towards practices was responsible for the breathtaking performances, I guess. Within days, the preparations for the fest began in the college.

Unlike last time, I was pretty much conscious of what I wanted to do. Music was what I saw myself doing. VISHESH was clear about how to make their performance a bench-mark and die-hard practice was the key.

The fest was twenty three days away as we began practicing the songs, finalized by Tushar. Having never been a part of a music band before, things were quite new for me. But lucky as I was, all of my folks were patient with me. Going by our preparations, we could bet our hard work was going to pay.

The fest was fourteen days away. Kunal started rehearsing the final song of the performance, while the rest 4 of us were playing our instruments.

"No, Kunal, the scale of the song should be higher. You're not getting any close to it." Tushar said to Kunal, just as he completed the first part. Kunal nodded and sang again, this time on a higher scale.

"Not like that. I suppose you have not heard it thoroughly??"

"Dude, I have heard and practiced it continuously for the past two hours. But I'll try again." Kunal said and tried another time. For once, twice, thrice, but no matter how many times he tried, he could not please Tushar.

Undoubtedly, Tushar had a grand sense of music, but with my knowledge, I really felt that Kunal was doing justice to the song. With every trial, Tushar's patience seemed to get extinguished, making him hyper. Kunal was still trying to refine himself until the moment Tushar blasted out on him.

"What the heck is so wrong with you, goddammit? Can't you just concentrate on what the song desires??" He shouted at the top of his voice. I was pretty shocked by his bizarre behaviour, but Kunal looked astonished. Silently, he kept staring into Tushar's now-blood -red eyes. Breaking the silence after a short while, he said, "No, I can't"

"What do you mean by 'I can't"?? You have to understand how important this is. Do you get it? I just can't let go of my band's performance because of a ......" Tushar stopped amid of his statement.

"Just because of a what?? Complete what you were about to say. Speak up." Kunal rebutted. It was Tushar's turn to keep mum now.

"Kunal, Tushar, forget it, guys. It's just that we need a break." Sandy and Vishal got up from their places, andstood between the two of them, Vishal signaled me to keep Kunal away.

"Kunal Sir, calm down. It is OK, we can sort it out peacefully." I said trying to pacify Kunal, as Vishal and

Sandy tried to bring Tushar back to his senses.

"No, Aryan. Let him finish. Tushar, let me make it clear that I too possess some intellect for music. "

"Yes, you do and that's why you end up singing like crap." Tushar said.

"What?? I'm the vocalist of this band and now you come and tell 'my voice is a crap."' It was all going wrong,mistaken. "I'm no way tolerating this bullshit." Kunal added, now turning away from Tushar and looking towards me. He was really hurt.

"Why are you telling this to him?? Say it on my face if you have guts." Tushar said.

"Tushar, what are you…." Sandy tried to intervene.

"Let me complete, Sandy. I just don't understand what you think of yourself. Oh man, peep out of this bloody room, we'll find another hundred singers like you. We'll get one for 'VISHESH' too. So, for God's sake, get lost. "

Kunal was baffled by all that he heard. Tushar was not just his band-mate, but a dear friend too. I noticed that even when I was not a part of 'VISHESH'. But, with those words Tushar said, he had crossed all his limits, brok all the bonds. It was then I realized that this was not a usual quarrel. It was going to have a massive impact.

Kunal gathered the courage to speak and said, "I can't believe you could say that." He looked towards the door.

"Kunal, don't be stupid. Wait a second." Vishal said.

"Yeah, Tushar Sir is just annoyed a lil. He did not mean anything." Even when I told that to Kunal, in my own heart, I wondered if I was lying.

"Ahm, I think I should leave now." Kunal's tone had turned from furious to forlorn.

"Thank you, so much. And take my words. We can perform without you, you'll see very soon."

"It makes no difference to me from now." Kunal said, smashing the dooras he left the practice room. Neither Sandy nor Vishal could stop him from leaving. But it was going to make a difference to Kunal, I knew. A huge difference!

After Kunal left, 'VISHESH' was shattered to smithereens.

Without a vocalist, our band became voiceless and soulless too. Tushar must have realized that, but he did not admit it in front of us. Vishal and I tried hard to convince but Kunal did not change his mind. Our attempts were not enough to bring Kunal back. But we had to perform at any cost. We could not step back. Our probe for a new vocalist took over us.

One day, I suggested, "There's a guy in my class whosings pretty well."

Tushar raised his eyebrows and said as an afterthought, "What's his name??"

"Rohit. But I wonder if he'll be willing to perform, but hopes are high."

"Hmmm, just give him a call." Tushar said anticipation in his eyes. I nodded.

Our search for a new vocalist got extinguished in the form of Rohit. I was happy when I introduced him to VISHESH, and even more happy that he would perform with us.

With Rohit's entry, destiny made someone else arrive-too, Manav. I was aware of the fact that Manav and Rohit were best friends.

But what came as a bolt of blue for me was Manav knew how to play guitar and convinced Tushar telling him that he would willingly buy a bass guitar. His achievement of getting a bass guitarist for VISHESH made Tushar's happiness burst at the seams, which meant my 'favourite' Manav became a part of our band.

The six of us started practicing wholeheartedly. My job was to provide bass, but given that 'VISHESH' had found a bass guitarist, things began to get rough for me. Yes, I knew well he was not really fond of me, and neither was I. But I loved music more than I hated Manav. And I could bear him for the sake of VISHESH's performance.

I had never imagined that Manav's entry could put my presence in shade. But it did. Needless to say, myexistence in 'VISHESH' was inversely proportional to his growing importance.

Manav had an upper hand over me, so more or less I was snubbed as 'no longer required'. It was not something I felt, but something they all made me realize. Whatever I did, they criticized it. Even my friendship with Kunal had begun to bother the thick-headed Tushar, overnight.

What VISHESH wanted from me had become a riddle wrapped up in enigma, which was no way easy to figure out.

Even after Tushar said to me, "We're practicing, you can sit over and see where ever you can manage to give some score." I tried every bit to retain my position. 'To give some score' was the only consolation I was given. But, for me, everybody's behavior prevaricated. They stopped reacting, let alone suggesting something to me. I had never seen such a sea change. The worst fell upon when I started feeling like I was not even present in that practice room. Nobody even bothered to talk to me.

I tried to win their confidence by providing lead background from the keyboard, but I was taken aback when they said, "It sounds like cacophony." Even though I knew well that convincing them was of no use, I did not give up. But, every attempt I made went in vain. Absolutely futile. I had become a toy to mock at. While I sat there every day alone watching them practice, overlooking my presence, Manav and Rohit were over the moon. Whatsoever I played or suggested, they hardly missed any opportunity to ridicule it. But, my heart got pierced when I over-heard Tushar said to Manav, "When will we get rid of this prick? Can't he just realize that he's hardly needed anymore?" Those words took life out of me. People I called 'friends', stabbed my back and gave me nothing except betrayal.

That day, I completely realised what I meant for 'VISHESH'. I meant an irritation, a pain in the neck. I realized I could be anything but not a stalker. The same band which had welcomed me with open arms, made me feel like an extra, recluse stalker. An outsider! I did not watch their performance, and just ran away.

That day, either my patience gave up or my conscience woke up. I told them "I won't be a waste-of-time, distraction in your practice sessions any longer". I plucked out the wires out of my keyboard, threw them in front of them and walked off. "Good riddance", I heard Manav say aloud, just as I stepped out. The invisible bond that stood between 'VISHESH' and me got converted to an invisible barrier which could not be crossed, no matter what I tried. Whatever I was scared of, turned into reality. I could feel Kunal's hurt. That night, my relationship with 'VISHESH' came to an end. End in its most tragic forms.

For life goes on!!

* * *

I did not want to return back to college, but Pulkitforced me to come. I tried to hide, to run, but he would never allow me to. He made me understand that I could not escape for longer and staying idle at home will only worsen things. At college, everyone was engrossed in things they loved. I was thrown out of mine.

Music was my craving. It helped me think and everything else seemed like mere options. I tried to get involved in an event or the other, but nothing helps when heart is elsewhere. But, I had to pose happy and unaffected, making my classmates or acquaintance believe that I could do well without 'VISHESH'. I wanted to watch them perform and applaudfor them, so that people don't deem me as a limping loser.

On the second day of the fest, when 'VISHESH' was about to perform, destiny had another drill prepared for me to pass, Pulkit and I were assigned the duty of managing the backstage itself.

Thrown out from VISHESH was not alone enough to

hurt me, Tanya's undying support for her 'best friend' Manav did the rest. I often doubted if she could not see that she was not a best friend to Manav who never missed any opportunity to flaunt her and flirt publicly with her. Why

Do I have to see her while he was ready to perform in my place? How badly I wished I was in his place for more than one reasons.

And why she was so oblivious of his intentions and even when she supported venom, she looked harmless which bothered me even more.

While Tushar, Vishal, Sandy, Rohit and Manav were excited for their performance, I wanted to run away from there to a distant place where I could not take a single glance at them.

But at exteriors, I tried to maintain composure. I could see an igniting spark in their eyes, where mine dwelled in pain. When I saw Manav notice me, I signaled a thumbs-up and passed a wide smile to him. They went ahead to perform. I took everything in my stride and then tried to get occupied in some activity, so that I did not get time to feel sick.

March 31st, 2009

* * *

The final day of the fest brought me face to face with many things. At 8:00 pm., it turned really dark, but the luminosity of the lights made every corner of the college gleam.

"Buddy, let's go that side." Rajat said, as we watched the show.

"Hmmm. Something wrong here??" I questioned, still looking at the engrossing play being performed.

"Not actually. But from there, the view will be a better." Rajat said. I was in no mood to protest, so we proceeded to the location he wanted. Just as we reached there, a girl emerged from a group of juniors and advanced towards Rajat.

After they shook hands, passed smiles, and exchanged eye-to-eye ciphers, Rajat introduced her as Parul. From a couple of months, I too had heard that Rajat a junior girl called Parul were smitten. But it was the first time, I was meeting her. So, by now I knew why my friend was so desperate to come to this side.

"Ohh. So Rajat Sir, what took you so long to travel

across twenty metres??"Parul asked him, exercising her, typically girl-friend rights on him.

"Actually, we liked it more there, so..." Rajat said, teasing her back.

"Ohoho! Poor you, I guess."

I stared at the stage, waiting for the play to begin, as Pulkit was part of it. , without disturbing the 'love birds', while they enjoyed pulling each other's legs. Unfortunately, it was two to three performances away, Pulkit informed me over a text. Quite soon they realized that he had a friend present there too. They involved me too, cracking few jokes about the performance carried out.

"Sir, that girl in blue is my room-mate and best friend." Parul told me pointing towards the announcer, just as a performance got wind up.

I wondered how to react to that. So, I smiled back and said a mild 'okay' to her. Before I could make any analysis over her appearance, she stepped down completing her job. Ms. Blue appeared on the stage a couple of times, after each performance. She was far and so could not make out how she exactly looked, but I could say she was not utterly fair, but neither that dark in complexion. As it appeared, she resembled Parul, but only shorter than her. Her command over the language I dreaded from the years was definitely impressive.

"Sir, my friend wants to come here, but she is a bit hesitant to come." Parul said to me, as the performance got over. I nodded and thought for a while. Hesitating? Do I bite, I wondered. May be a stranger was the reason for her discomfort.

"Oh! That's OK, I won't mind leaving if you want. " I said, still wondering about the awkward situation that made me perceive myself as a 'woman-eater'.

"No. you got me wrong." She said, protesting.

"Then, guys??" I asked her back, as she made another

secretive gesture to her 'potential' boyfriend.

Following her expressions, Rajat said, "Dear, you go and check if your friend is searching for you. Let me explain."

"So, tell me lover-boy, what did your beloved just try to say??" I winked at him, just as he turned to me.

He blushed for a second and said, "Well, she meant that someone's being in great demand."

"Who?? Demand as in??"

"For some girl. The same one who's feeling nervous to come in front of you."

"Hold on, man, what does that imply??" I asked him as I felt something fishy going on.

Before he could answer me back, Parul arrived with this 'I'm very scared of you' chic. She was the same announcer Parul told me about a few minutes ago. After she greeted Rajat and then she looked at me, but fell silent. Finally after five seconds, I said a 'hi' to her to ease out the silence.

"Sirat, he's my friend, Aryan." Rajat said, as she smiled, looking straight in to my eyes. The dark eye make-up she had worn looked relevant and was fairly noticeable.

"I really loved you at the stage. Awesome." Parul said, pampering her best friend. Only girls, I suppose, are the species who are capable of promoting public display of affection so easily.

"Yuppi. Thank you." She answered, as Parul looked at me with expecting eyes.

"Uhm. She's right. Nice job, Sirat." I complemented her as well.

"Sirat." She smiled and then added in her extra-sweet tone, "Thanks a lot, Sir. Now I believe that it went well."

"'Now you believe', huh?? So, Ms. Sirat does not believe my words." Parul said, pulling her legs.

"May be I don't." She chuckled, as Rajat grinned. Witty best friend and giggling boyfriend are not too a pleasing combination. Poor Parul.

Then Sirat added, "No idiot, it's that you praise mefor everything I do, but now I have got one confirmation."

The way she teased Parul, it was quite unbelievable that this same girl was feeling shy to come in front of me, just a couple of minutes ago.

Finally, it was my best friend and his group's turn to perform. I had seen the rehearsals a couple of times, but their act was magical enough to keep everyone's eyes glued to the stage for the next few minutes.

"Aryan." Sirat said as the performance ended. I threw her a look, "Aryan Sir, you played an instrument in the fresher's party, didn't you??"

"I did, but how do you know, you two are from??" "Computers department." She said, as we both smiled. "Oh good."

So, after a few minutes, she asked "So, did you perform in the fest??"

"No, not this time." I said, wishing she would not dig in to the matter anymore which are buried in my heart.

"But why n..." She said as I made an excuse, without letting her complete that I had an urgent call to make. I walked aside and called up Pulkit to ask him, if he could make it faster. But, the noise around made it difficult for me to understand what he spoke.

I told Rajat that Pulkit was waiting for me somewhere, so I headed away from them, biding them adieu.

I left because I dreaded that Sirat might ask me something that I would not want to answer. After all, I was not answerable to the girl who had flown in, just a couple of minutes ago. And the last thing I wanted to happen was ruining my own mood to give some strange chic a topic for gossip and Pulkit to reach them.

Life after the fest rolled on to the usual mugging up

schedule, internals, and results. Our date-sheet for the fourth semester exams came out the following week. Yes, it was like the toughest semester so far. But, I had done enough in the fourth semester to ensure that my preparations was next to nil. But my only consolation was that, the exams were almost a month away. So, from the next morning itself, I made sure that my books had rule life for a month at least.

I was supposed to devote myself to the ocean of engineering books. But what life brought turned my world upside down. The sight I found Tanya's head on Manav's shoulder as I entered my vacant classroom devastated me. Were they not just friends?

And if they were, which friends sit like that?

Her proximity with him not only startled me, but I just left the room saying, "I'm sorry."

I heard Tanya saying something from behind, but I did not turn back. May be she just ran for an assurance that I would not tell anybody what my eyes saw. I wanted to grab and punch that Manav's face, but which guy would let go of Tanya. More importantly, who was I to do that.

Later that evening, I saw Tanya's call flashing on my cell phone. But I had no courage to pick up. Why the hell was she calling me now? To mince salt over my wounds?

I cursed life for making the guy named 'Manav' a part of my life. Firstly, he snatched my dream from me, and then the girl I saw in my dreams. What more he want to do? And the worst why could not I help it even when he stole from me everything I cared for.

As I did not answer any of her calls, I saw her text. In a moment I deleted without reading. I wanted to reply but I did not write back anything. Nothing was left on my part. But, that sight tortured me. I thought of her smile, and the next moment I thought of the reason behind her smile. It was

Manav. Life, ehh was not a great thing, I guess!

As days passed by, I could find the budding couple everywhere. Manav never left Tanya. The moment I saw them prepare for the exams together, I could not concentrate at all. Most of the times, my mind was entangled with her thoughts. And she had entangled herself with somebody else. I often doubted if Manav really loved Tanya. "He could not as much as I did", I used to mumble this line like a typical bollywood movie.

Just a week was left for the exams to commence and I hardly cared. I used to lock myself in my room, telling mom that I was studying, but all nights, I kept looking at the walls. Though I tried my best to hide it, Pulkit noticed how I was ruining myself. He asked me the reason that disturbed me, but I did not tell him even a word. But he figured out what bothered me somehow I guess, and pushed me to study. Perhaps, my learning power was lost. My mind could not grasp anything, no matter how much I strived. . I scheduled myself in the ocean of engineering books. When the exams began, it seems like the universal time unit had got condensed secretly. Days seemed shorter than ever.

And it looked like the fourth one was the shortest semester of my engineering life and the hardest one. Exams wrapped up in a blink of eye, but that was what I desired honestly. And I hardly knew how I performed.

The summer of 2009 was supposed to be different. Being an engineering students for two years, the curriculum asked us to get summer internships. I was looking forward for it for more than one reason. This was the chance to acquire skills that could help us get acquainted with the trends of IT industry. Like many of my classmates, Pulkit and I had successfully got ourselves registered in one of the reputed institutes in Chandigarh.

Apart from academic motives, I wanted to use this

opportunity to erase Tanya from my memory, anyhow. I hoped Chandigarh could help me do that. I had never been away from home, and Pulkit decided to stay at his uncle's house. This bothered mom at first instance, but I placated her that Rajat and I were going to share the room. On my end, I was happy that I was going away. When you are 20, things like these fancy you, I guess.

The first day of my internship was quite inspiring, as we were brought face to face about the why's and how's of the IT world.

Impressed as I was, I made up in my mind that I would work really hard and try to make the most of the opportunity. But the very next day, we were divided into different batches. Surprisingly, Pulkit and I were allotted different batches. Something we literally hated! Though we tried to get a solution, but that internship, things were going to be really different I believe.

Despite of a great beginning, I did not know when things started appearing again messy to me. I was free most of the time and kept thinking how life took its course in the past one year. Tanya's glances haunted me day and night. But every time I thought of her, another face rolled up in front of me. And every time Manav returned, the images of my failure reverted to me. It had been six long months when I was thrown out of VISHESH, but every night I stayed awake thinking about the reasons that separated me from VISHESH. Yes, I missed something way more than Tanya, it was music.

One fine day while I was returning home, I heard a guy playing guitar in the park that faced the institute. I listened to him, it seemed that all my fatigue of that day disappeared in just five minutes. And not just the fatigue, but a huge load from my mind got lightened. It had to be, because I had found the answer to a question that had frustrated me from long. Perhaps, I could not save my place in VISHESH because of my inability to play guitar. Perhaps, learning guitar could be the panacea that I was finding. I walked to the guy and asked from where he learnt playing guitar, he told me about a music academy that was situated just 100 meters away from my internship institute. I was thrilled by the answer and walked up to the academy. That moment when I filled the admission form, I wondered for a second "whether I was making a hurried decision"? But today, I know it was the best decision that I could ever make in my life. Joining the music academy, things in my life took a U-turn. Though it took a while for me to touch base with guitar, but my past was hurting enough to prevent me from giving up.

In fact, my instructor was a man of patience. He had done expertise in making the newcomers getting familiar with guitar. After I discovered that playing a guitar had become my need, I bought an acoustic guitar. My passion for guitar almost changed everything. Yes, I was getting passionate about something that won't hurt me. There was no more gloom in my nights, I slept smiling. The more I played guitar, the more I craved for it. I realized that learning to play guitar was the feast I would trade my life for.

However, my attendance at the internship was falling. The internship really looked like an imposition. Pulkit often budged me about it, but all his efforts were in vain. On my part, it was hard to miss out on my passion, but I tried to show my face to the tutors at least twice a week. But I compensated for my heart by playing guitar till late in night. Though, my roommates never openly complained about the disturbance my new love created for them, I could figure their discomfort.

But the question was how do I stop myself? Giving up what I had been dying for was going to be blunder. So, I decided to practice guitar in the veranda outside my room till morning. Finally, things worked out well.

During my stay in Chandigarh, the internship inclined

to become a second fiddle, and guitar a real charm. But I did not give up any chance enjoying with my friends. The second time we went for camping in the outskirts, they asked me to take along my guitar. And it was an amazing experience.

As our internship was about to end, we were asked to develop projects in the computer language we had learnt during the internship. My development skills were simply out of question, so I asked Rajat to make me part of his team, who agreed without a second thought. Much like Rajat, our other teammate was super intelligent and super hardworking, which proved to be a great help.

Apart from discovering my love for guitar, Chandigarh succeeded in bringing a sea change in me. Being my first experience of staying away from home taught me to manage things on my own. Fortunately, I had started giving a thought before I say anything and not ended up saying everything that I thought. One of the big lessons of life indeed!

But what it changed the most was my perception of things. My interaction with my guitar tutor there had rooted in me a strange confidence about music. I remember his words so well when he said, "everything worth gettingis never placed on the discount shelves."

College started on 2nd September for the third year. And life rolled back to normalcy. No more night-outs, no more fun rides, no more day-long Guitar practices only boring classes were what we were left with. Classes, labs, and then of course the new stretched out speeches by every professor to wake us up.

In the first week, none of the professors left without giving us a ten minute sermon. Everyone advised the same thing that we had to open our eyes and start preparing for the placements, GATE, CAT, or wherever we wanted to land in the near future. On our end, it meant nothing more than nice way to kill time. Words like 'constructive', 'expertise' are no big deal when you enter third year. Are they? Like always, our class kept up with the 'bunking theory' to balance out the equations with back-breaking lectures.

Once after attending the sixth lecture, I was returning home, when I met Sirat. She was outside the library the place I never been after I cleared my first year. Her white colored suit was fairly visible from a distance. It suited her well. According to me, white is the color that suits everyone.

"What's the crowd here for??" I asked as she advanced towards me.

"Actually, they have put up the list of new additional books for each year. So..?" she said as I nodded.

"Oh, the lecturers don't tell you all this in the class."
"They do. But who lends an ear to them??" She chuckled.

I gave her a look. She added "I mean, ultimately we'll have to end up coming in the library only to get them issued, isn't it?."

"Yeah, I guess. And do tell me, if I can help." "Sir, actually, you can." "OK. Tell me."

"Sir, do you have the book on Database Systems by Navathe?" She asked and waited for me to answer. After a couple of seconds, she added, "I promise I'll return it just after this semester."

"Not that, my mind was somewhere else. I'll look for it at home and let you know." I wondered how I would tell her.

"Sure, and if it helps ask Rajat Sir to inform me about it through Parul. Only if you don't mind." she said.

"Oh. I would."

"What?? Would you mind or would you tell??" she asked with a confused expression.

"The latter, of course." I said. Her lips converted into a smile.

The next day, I said to Rajat, "Hey, convey something to Sirat."

"Whattttttttt do you want to convey, man?????" He asked me as if I was disclosing the hugest of secrets.

"This! Just a book, buddy." I said as I gave him the book and made it clear that she had asked for it. Poor gossiper lost his chance, I smirked.

"Ohh. I thought that you too." He said and winked.

"Wait a second. Don't you dare tell me what you thought?" I warned him. "And give it to Parul, she'll pass it on."

"Oh. Do you mind if I give it to Sirat directly??" He said teasingly.

"Well, not me. But someone else might." I shrugged.

"Who??"

"Parul." I said and laughed as Rajat made a disappointed face.

Music was growing in me, day by day. By now, I learnt one thing. If you want to be a part of something, find ways, or better create your own. Who knows there might be others who are waiting for a door to get opened, the one you build. If you want to dance, find platform. If you want to play sports, search for your mates, push them and go hit the courts. If you want to perform music, find your ways, your band may be out there and go for it.Just step ahead, because if you don't, you'll always stay in the same place. Don't wait for someone else to do something, you can't live without. Music was that thing for me, so I had to find the ways leading me to it. And if not find, then create them.

Not for a day or two, but I had given a deep thought to the venture of creating a music band on my own but considerable number of days. Risks, opportunities, necessities, Pros, cons, everything. And, in the most crucial decisions you have to ever make, your brain surrenders to your heart very often.

The most important thing about creating a music band meant converging all the members to certain point, which connects them. But for making that happen, the members should exist too. So, Target 1 was searching for people who could slog to stay together. And I was ready to plump any depths for it.

College's talent hunt helped me finding a guitarist. After Jatin won the instrumentals round, he precipitated in to my preference list. He accepted my offer without any second thought. There was another guy in my mind who had ranted at a friend's party about his drumming abilities.

But I was not pretty sure about him, because in parties like that, people often booze and do one of the two things: either exposing everything they had ever done or flaunting and claiming about everything they had never tried before.

I really wished he did not belong to the 2nd category. Somehow I found that guy. Though, the exercise included asking the uncountable people, who could be related to him in any possible ways. Some threw suspected looks at me. How do you react when a guy who never asked about a girl, probing excitedly about another guy? Exactly the same way.

Finally, all is well that ends well. I met him. Arpit. "Yes, I can play drums. But this band thing is too hi-fi for me."

"Hi-fi!! Oh come on. Be confident." I said.

"Hmm. But I don't possess a drum kit. So, seems quite tough."

"Look buddy. If I get confident about your drumming abilities, I'll get the drum kit arranged." I told him.

"Aryan, are you serious??"

"Do I look like I'm not?? Of course, I'm, but I need to get assured."

"OK."

I was ecstatic when Arpit told that he had a friend who could let him play his drums. "Who is this friend? I mean who would rarely take the risk of putting his drum-kit in the college." I asked Arpit as a matter-of-fact.

"That's right, but he's in the band called 'VISHESH',

Sandy."

"Sandy?"

"Yeah, and Sandeep actually, but he is just paranoid about being called by this name." Arpit continued talking, but I was under a shock for his previous statements. I mean, why was I destined to have close shaves with the set of people I wished to depart from this planet? Even though it was the need of the hour, I was reluctant to go back to those irritating faces and ask for anything. Even the minutest of favours from them was unforgivable. "I was wondering if I had heard about him." I said as an excuse,after Arpit shudder me from my dilemma.

"Are you really sure they'll allow us?" I asked him, trying to keep my expression as normal as I could.

"I suppose, and it's such a small thing that they won't take their hands off." he said, as I kept mum trying to figure out. I asked him, "Can't we find some other way out?"

Arpit tried to convince me by saying, "We won't get a drum-kit anywhere else in the college buddy. It won't take much time. And if we go ahead, it might make things easier for us, I guess." He made sense. I could not stand the stupidity of buying a drum-kit on the basis on assumptions. I had to think practically.

"Hmmm, so your friend won't say no to you?" I questioned him finally.

"In no case."

Arpit made a call to Sandy and like Arpit had said, it did not take much time to ask for what we wanted. Arpit directed us to the room, where we met Sandy and Tushar. In the first moment after we entered in, I was happy that at least the other two were not present. Rohit, undoubtedly, topped my order of preference when it came to disgust. While Arpit talked to them for a minute or two, I made sure I look totally occupied with my phone. Anything that could help me overlook their presence would do!

And then finally, Arpit played the drums for some 3-4 minutes. To be honest, he was not too good, but he was not that bad either and chances of finding someone else for drumming was rare. After we left the room, Arpit asked what was going in my mind.

I just said one sentence. "I'll get the drums."

At home, I could not reveal my new wish. A new drum kit required no less than 10000 bugs. So, it was out of question. Paying this amount when their son did not even know a, b, c of it!!!! My parents were not that credulous. But luckily, the way came out of the will. I heard of an orchestra group who intended to sell their drum kit. I checked that their drums were in good condition. On some bargaining, they agreed to trade it for Rs. 5400. I brought them home with dad's permission and of course his money. The very next evening, I called up Arpit. He disconnected the call and texted back:

"I'm at home for some urgent work. Can't pick ur call. Will call u wen I return after six days."

So, I had to prolong my wait for another six days. That was what I thought by then. Just six days!

Meanwhile, my meetings with Sirat became more frequent. Although, it could not be exactly called meetings, but stopping for a minute or two, while we passed nearby. She had floated away from my list of 'Ignorables' to the normal category.

All human beings have a tendency to plan everything in advance. Arpit would return in a week, Jatin is right here. We'll find a vocalist soon. I had laid a full-fledged plan in my mind. But God has his own ways to practice his powers. To ruin our plans! May be that's why he's the God and we are mere creatures.

Two days later, my result for fourth semester came out. I had scored a.........back log in the subject 'Microprocessors and Interfacing'.

Shock, distress, petrified - these words were just not enough to define what I felt when I saw that devastating web page. In those initial minutes of terror, things made no sense. How could I get a backlog?? The exam went OK, if not great but a backlog was the least I expected. The least I deserved.

Hundreds of thoughts took birth in my mind, none of them justifying the catastrophe rewarded to me. In my last three semesters, I had managed to score 75% easily. And now this disgrace was churning my interiors. There was no extent of what I was going through. I had no courage to tell mom and dad, but it was not tough for them to find out as I was at home. "What, the hell do you study in college?? Guitar chords, is it??"

"Is this what we get in return from our son, who was never been denied for anything so far??" I could not answer back the rage. I dared not to.

They were right. It could not go this way. May be they had the right to say this now but my heart did not pay consent when they even blamed music for this massacre of hopes.

Music can't be a fly in the ointment of success for any one. It is an inspiration in itself. At a corner of my mind I knew what ruined everything, I just did not want to reiterate Tanya story in my mind.

I saw an incoming call on my cell phone from Pulkit. I had already seen that he had managed to score a decent 72%. I did not want to congratulate someone when I had screwed up myself, so badly.

Moreover, I knew if I pick up the phone mom would ask about his result and I would not want to say "He scored 72percent in the exam that made me flunk." Her reaction on hearing that would kill me silently. Parents like making comparisons, only when their own children are on the losing end.

I disconnected the phone and switched it off. I did not

feel like talking to anyone. More than mom's bitter words,dad's silence pinched me. I packed my guitar and the newly acquired drums and placed them in the storeroom. I locked its door.

It was Sunday. In a way, it was good. I did not want to go to college. But I did not want to stay back. I just wanted to run away. I was almost twenty and I had never failed in one exam before.

I had often consoled many friends not to lose heart in such a situation. But saying is easy, only saying is. Even in the darkest moment, I thought of ending it up at once. But the very next second, my family came to my mind. I had already hurt them before, they did not deserve this. I just could not ruin it for them anymore.

On Monday morning, I did not want to go to college. But, I had no courage to look into my parent's eyes. So, I left for college. Even on the way, I thought of skipping it. But, for how long could I sit back and sulk??

I went to the college, thinking that I had to return there one day or another. Inside the college, the ambiance was pretty normal. For the first time in 2.5 years, I reached my classroom before anyone else. Very few asked me about the result. Only two to three. I assumed the rest already knew what I was up to. But when I was correct?? People did not ask me, because then they'll have to tell their score too.

There was a mass backlog in MICROPROCESSOR & INTERFACING. Around thirty five students out of sixty had failed.

Even though, I could not go and announce this at home, but it deceased my mourning. Failure anyways means a failure. But there's a bigger truth- nothing heals like time. It heals everything that makes you suffer. To my relief, situation at home was getting normal. In college, everyone's state was alike, except some big-headed geniuses. Consequently, I started attending all the lectures. I did not roam out to save myself from the embarrassment that I had to face after disclosing my results to anyone.

I would pass through the corridors only twice a day from college gate to our block in the morning and the way back after dispersal. I was going home one day, when unfortunately Sirat stuck me. As always, she appeared out of nowhere. I thought, I would say a "hii" and escape down from there, before she ask about anything else. About my results!

She had borne in her mind that I was a studious guy. She had even admitted this once I came across her in the corridors. I did not want my impression to get faded and being snubbed as a 'dumb failure'. It had always bothered me.

"Hii." she said, before I did.

"Hii." I said and acted like I needed to rush up.

"Is there something wrong??"

"No. Seems like that??" I asked, unmindfully. "Sort of."

"Nopes." I said, straight away. And then added, "I need to leave, dear. I'll catch up later."

"Sure."

"Please don't mind that, Bye, take care."

"You too. And don't worry, some exams in life have a re-appear option too."She said.

I left the next second, without giving a thought. I was happy she did not ask me anything. But, wait a minute. The last sentence she spoke?? What did she mean?? I'm sure if I would have been out of my mind not to understand when she spoke the last line. May be, she already knew about my results. Whatever!

Internal exams appeared up soon. I had a bigger reason to score well this time. It's amazing to see how your perspective about everything around you change after just one setback. I worked as hard as I could. I threw Tanya thing out of my mind completely. And it got paid. I scored well in almost all the subjects.

My performance not only pulled me out of the miserable post-failure phase, but also helped a lot to improve the condition at home. Everything rolled on to usual. I was relieved that it did. Though I never told anyone, there was a void in my life. Day and night, I missed my keyboard and guitar. Every time I looked at mom and dad, I thought of asking if I could get my necessities back. But the fear of getting a blunt 'no' pulled me back.

After a couple of days, when I found them immensely happy, since one of my cousin's marriage got fixed. I roasted the opportunity to my own benefit. Initially, they said a 'no', but I knew they could not deny me for long.

They agreed. I promised them about not letting music affect my academic performance.

I got my guitar and keyboard from the store-room. Holding each of them in my hands after more than three weeks, I realized how much they meant to me. More than ever before, I valued them even more now. My most prized possessions!

Arpit called me once to ask about the drums and practice. I told him that I had bought them, but I could not show a green signal for practice. I did not want another black-out at home again. So, I asked him to wait till the post-semester vacations.

The final practical's started and the semester exams began soon for the fifth semester. I was asked by my family to put music on hold and restrict myself to the course books. It was an order, so I had no other option. I did as they asked me to. The last I wanted was disappointing them by earning another stain on my degree. My focus was on exams and nothing else. By god's grace, exams went off really well.

The sixth semester started on 2nd February. Quite earlier than the usual! In a way, it was good for us. The college fest was meant to be organized by March's extreme end,so I was happy to get more time for the preparations.

Formulating a music band was not a silk cake walk. It needed time and patience.

Not wasting much time, I met Arpit as soon as I could.

"Yeah, but we had just made a plan and performing on the stage is completely different thing, Aryan."

"It is, for sure. But everything needs a start. This might be ours. Just make one thing clear, are you willing to play??" I asked him.

"I'm, indeed. But you should have consulted me once, before buying the drums. Buddy, I can't pay Rs.5000 right now." Arpit grumbled.

"Oh so that is the case. Look, I have not asked you to pay me at this moment. I'm not running anywhere, neither are you. "

"Hmmm. But I'm not that skilled, man. The entire college will be in front of us, noticing every move of ours. "

"That's what we want at the end of the day. Don't we??" I said as he nodded.

"If we practice, we can improve. We all can." I continued, trying to instill some confidence in him.

"Yup. But still...!"

"Don't worry. We'll cope-up with everything.... together.

"I assured him.

"Crap it, shit shit..!" I jumped out of the car, after hearing a collapsing sound. To my fear, it was the sound of the smash between the left back light and the college's boundary wall. The back light had smeared into pieces of broken glass. It was around six in the wintry evening. And if you're scratching your head wondering what I was doing there, the answer is: I was returning home after putting the drums in Arpit's hostel room. But when did life plan to become easy on me?

There I was, stuck like another day, staring at the pieces

of broken glass which glow the back light of the car 2 minutes back. I looked around to check if anyone noticed. I could not spot anyone known outside the college. Thank God, I whispered. But the very next moment, God proved two things:

One, I was wrong.

Two, God did not deserve any 'thanks'.

My heartbeat raced up as somebody tapped at my shoulder. I turned around to find Sirat. Hats off, Mr. Fate. If there was someone who could get listed amongst people making unexpected appearances at all weirdly awkward situations, it had to be undoubtedly her.

"You?? What have you been doing here??" I asked her angrily, in reflex. She was not expected to be there in that dark. The next moment, I hoped that my statement did not make me look protective about her.

"Sir, I should be the one asking this. I'm returning from home. If there is anyone whose presence needs to be questioned, it is you." she said. I thought of something to tell her, as she added, "Not willing to go home??"

"No nothing, some private work at college." I said, hoping she had not spotted me, putting a stain on my dad's prized possession. May be she had not.

"Ohoho. So by 'Private work', Mr. Aryan means bumping his car into the college building." she said, clearing all my doubts and laughed aloud. Was it even funny?? Not to me, certainly.

"So you saw it, right? Then why pretended like you did not?" I grumbled.

"Because I thought you might confess that. But how could you do that with annoying strange lass. Isn't it??" She taunted.

In no sense, I was going to explain her on how important she is when I was already messed up.

"I would have, if that helped. It just happened. I left

the clutch abruptly while driving back."

"Uhm, one can see well. I need to walk back. But anyways be ready..." Before she could complete, her cell-phone rang. So, she moved away. I did not speak as she has gestured me not to. So, she started moving towards the college gate. She waved bye, but I did not speak as she has gestured me not to. By the time she hung up the phone, she was already meters away from me.

"Be ready for what, ma'am?" I asked her as she hung up.

"For what your dad will do to his son." She said, turning back for a moment and disappeared.

"Huh, Over smart girl", I murmured to myself.

Not Again..!

* * *

By now, I had three people prepared in my team. The drummer- assumingly. The guitarist- yes. And I-more than anyone else. We had sought the permission for practice after the college timings. I could play guitar, but only to an extent. However, my long relationship with keyboard had taught me enough to look fair with it. So, I opted to play keyboard at the stage.

No matter how our practice trials started but of course, the basic necessity was yet to be fulfilled. The pivot of the band, the vocalist was still missing. And I could not shut my eyes to the fact that finding the voice of our band was the absolute need of the hour.

We had put up notices on every notice-board of our college. Whichever may be the College, Cafeteria always accounts to be the most flooded place, visited by maximum number of students. Keeping that in mind, I had converted half-a-chart into the notice highlighting our probe, for cafeteria's notice board. We had set a date for auditioning the interested ones, if any. Owing to my impatient nature, I wanted it to be as early as possible. But Arpit insisted that we should give appropriate amount of time to the students to know, think, and decide.

On the day of auditions, the day turned out to be a fateful one. We received good response and variety of options. 9 people came up for the auditions. Though most of the candidates preferred Hindi songs, some sang English songs. Even two guys, amongst those who turned up, could rap. Some of them were really OK. Some were a bit lacking our parameters.

But we succeeded in finding someone eligible, quenching our band's thirst, Sameer. His superfluous voice made us choose him over his "not-yo-yo" type looks. We were not judging a beauty pageant after all, the three of us knew.

However, the drummer had a craze about growing extra-long hair and matched them up with the weirdest kind of beard any one ever chose to keep. No one in our band could claim to look like a rockstar. Yes, we did not even possess the kind of faces only a mother can love, but we all managed to look fine. Good music does not come with the compulsion of particular looks, thankfully.

So target one was achieved. I had found all my 'Anmol Ratna's'. We could hit the practice ground now.

We started practicing from the very next day. I had arranged the mike and amplifier from a choir. Among e four of us, Sameer and Jatin were junior. My past experience had shown me well how hierarchy could contribute in ruining peace between the members. So, I had borne in my mind to take special care that nobody felt abandoned in any sense. I battled for one more thing -If my band-mates would support my choice of playing keyboard. They did. I could give bass & lead both, with my new keyboard.

We choose a song by everyone's consent. Not only it was a mood setter, its scale suited Sameer's voice perfectly. I was with Jatin once, when I asked him, "You really think an acoustic guitar can work. I mean it's just a beginner's guitar, you know. "

"Sort of, but it will. I've seen many people performing with this only." He said.

"Of course, let's see." He had won the talent hunt last year. So he definitely knew more about Guitar, I thought.

With further practice, things started taking a turn around. When we practiced we realized the scale or volume of the guitar was somewhat low or possibly the beat of the drum was too high, loud enough to suppress the tune of the guitar. We tried practicing for another three and half hours. But all in vain.

I spoke up, "wait wait. Everyone, hold on. I think we should concentrate on the Guitar. It's not properly audible. "

"Exactly. Aryan, didn't you suggest Jatin to get the amplifier? One amp is just not sufficient for keyboard, guitars and mike." Arpit said and turned towards Jatin "They'll really help in raising the power." Jatin did not speak.

"It would not be easy to work without them." Arpit spoke again.

"Hmm. I agree. Look Jatin, you have seen it yourself. You can reconsider the amplifier, once again." I suggested him.

"Well, I think guitar is the necessity here, not the amps on the stage."

"Is that the only reason stopping you from buying it??" I asked him back.

"Yes, with a couple of others, Inexplicable."

"But, you can adjust, we'll need them for the future too."

Arpit said trying to convince him. Jatin hardly responded. I did not want any rift. So, I interrupted in between. We decided to call off the practice for the next day.

Inside, I was optimistic that I won't let the absence of some amplifiers become any ordeal in my dream. I was confident that we might do it without the amps too.

On the next session of practice, Sameer turned out to

be in order. He had to sing along the sync of the instruments.

"Can you sing the song without any one of us playing??" Arpit asked him.

"Like without any rhythm or beats??" Sameer said.

"Yes dear. Just like humming. It might help us. Don't worry there is no sword hanging over your head." I said.

He sang the song for us and honestly, he did complete justice to the song.

"Alright then, here we go and start up together." I said, smiling at him. How content I felt when I heard him. His voice had filled the practice room with an unusual radiance.

After a while, Sameer turned up to the Arpit and said, "Sir, I think the sound of the drums is too high. Can you beat them a little slower??"

"Of course!"

He continued to sing again. But the beat of the drums got louder than before.

"Play a bit softly." He signaled again to Arpit.

"I'm doing it from a while." Arpit replied. We jumped back to the practice. After half an hour, all of a sudden Arpit stopped playing and stepped out from there.

"You were right, man. This beat is too frantic." He said calmly but his face was red, I observed indicating a sense of tension.

"Hey, hey, sit buddy. Don't worry." I tried to make him comfortable as Jatin passed him some water to drink.

"I may be playing awful." He said to me worriedly and then looked at Sameer.

"That's not true, sir. Really, that isn't." Sameer answered to him starkly.

"He's right, Arpit. We are all trying hard to improve." I said.

"Hmmm, can we join tomorrow if you don't mind?

It's too late." Arpit asked.

"Yup. It's close to 11. I should go home too. We'll catch up tomorrow." I said and then turned towards Jatin.

"Can we meet tomorrow if you have a free lecture. I have some guitar-related queries, Sirrrrrr!!" I said, making a childlike innocent face.

"Ahh!! I'll let you know if I have one. But I can't promise anything." He said in a tone that only the cruelest teacher can possess. I pouted.

"Oho. Stop making faces like that. I'll call you." He said and we laughed. So did Arpit and Sameer.

We practiced for four to five days and continuously failed to in synchronize with each other. For me, it had become a routine to attend college, go back home for an hour or two and then return back again for the practice sessions. It is amazing how we all get used to the joyful things in life. The practice timings were the part of the day which I used to eagerly wait for.

Four of us were practicing that night, when Sameer told Arpit politely that he was missing the beats. But Arpit seemed quite occupied.

We continued somehow, until Sameer went a bit annoyed with Arpit and said "Sir, I just told you something. And we can at least expect you to concentrate and follow."

I hoped Arpit would now concentrate and improve to play the beats carefully. But he did not pay any heed and rather behaved in a very blatant manner.

"You better concentrate on your singing, Mr. Vocalist." he suspended Sameer off. In return Sameer kept staring at him.

I intervened "Arpit, it happens buddy. Some beats are getting missed." Luckily, my intervention helped the situation to cool down.

Arpit and I decided to listen to the original version of the song again, so that we could trace out the missing beats.

Unlike before, Arpit gave proper attention before playing. He tried harder and harder but it didn't work at all. I hoped it would do. In the end, he gave up.

"Crap! What the hell am I doing here, if I can't even rattle this stupid drum??" He said clamorously. It seemed as if he had posed that question to himself. He threw away the beating sticks and ran away, towards the door.

Not again, I thought to myself. I could not let anything go wrong splitting this band into nuggets.

I chased him. Rest of the two followed. I stopped Arpit pulling his arm forcefully.

"What happened, man, all of a sudden??"

"Aryan, you are asking me what happened?? Can't you just see?? "

"See what?? Tell me what is wrong. Did anybody say something wrong to you??" I asked him patiently. He didnot answer any thing and rather tried to release his arm. I budged him to speak but he did not.

"You owe me an answer goddammit. You can't leave like this. Are you listening to me??" I shouted at him for the first time.

"Fine then, I'm tired of bearing all this. I can't handle it anymore." I expected him to speak out whatever he had in his head but he did not and became silent again. I realized I had to evoke him again.

"What does 'it' mean?? Speak up for yourself man. What is bothering you so much??"

"This criticism. I can barely see you guys playing so well. I'm just spoiling things, driving them to the worst. I had told you earlier that I might not be able to match up with you guys. Then why, why did you involve me??"

"There is no point in brooding. I know you had made yourself clear. But I also told you that things can take a better turn. This is a chance for all of us." I said

"Whatever it is. But I just want to get out of this shit." What so ever he said, he raised my heckles.

"Then fuck off." I screamed and left the place.

What else do I answer a guy who called my dream crap? It was for the first time in life that I used such a word. Even when I said it, I was sure that it would not be possible for us to perform anything together.

But Jatin & Sameer's convincing power made the impossible happen. They brought us together at least for once. However, it proved to be another fiasco. Even after we gave up our ego, we could not carry on for too long. There was hardly any spot of compatibility and coordination between us. We gave up just a week before the college fest.

Two days later, I decided to lock up the place where we used to practice. It was hardly of any avail to me now, so I went to return back the keys to the ma'am-in-charge. Spotting any professor in the college premises except the lecture hall is no less than a tedious task. Finally, half a round of the whole college made me find the need of the "endangered" species. She was involved in a decoration team. I returned back the keys, avoiding any big conversations.

The moment I turned to march back, Sirat was standing in front of me, with her trademark cheesy smile.

She said "Hiiiiii." Her "Hiii" was as cheesy as she was. "Hii." I replied and kept it short.

"What happened?? Did you just proposed someone and got spanked in return??" she said and chuckled. I gave her a disgusted look, my trademark was enough to make her realize that I was in nooooo mood to appreciate her self-entertaining jokes.

"Oh. I'm sorry."

"That's OK. May I leave??" I asked her and started moving away without her consent. Must have been rude. But thank God!

I had taken just a few steps, when I realized something. She had been running slowly towards me matching my steps. "Sir, Sir, Sir. Would you mind if I take your two minutes??"

I did not rebel. "OK sure." I said.

"I just wanted to say 'thank you' for the book you lent me. I know it's stupid of me saying it after a long time."

"Never mind. You're welcome"

"Hmmm. But not like this." she said sheepishly.

"Then like what?" I questioned.

She offered me some chocolates.

"Oh thank you. But I don't like chocolates."

"Realllllllllllllllllyy??" she said it over dramatically, making me wonder as if I had said no to oxygen.

"But they are good for health."

"Oh realllllly" I said imitating her. "So who discovered this fact?? Ms. Sirat??"

"No. But seriously, they are good. Do you know people who eat chocolates can survive more than those who do not??"

"In that case, you are immortal." I said.

"Shhh!! How did you just find out my secret?? Please don't tell it to anyone." She whispered.

"Sorry. Won't be able to help much in this." I teased back. She pouted. I said "wait let me see. Actually I can, if..."

"If what?????"

"If I get two of them" I said, winking and pointed towards the chocolates. She gave them to me and said, "But in only one condition, if we can share them." How much did she love chocolates? We shared them.

I was not exactly in a really joyful mood, but I was feeling much better. Then she asked me something which I did not expect her to. She asked "So, why are you upset??"

"Am I?? Are you kidding me??"

"No not kidding this time." Her expressions were rarely serious, but at that moment, hell, they were.

"It is something related to the music band. It did kind of split up, na??" She answered her own question.

"It never got formed." I said.

"But what happened??"

I kept mum.

"It's OK. I should not be intruding so much, being an outsider" She said.

"No no, it is not like that. Actually due to various reasons, we could not fall into the proper sync."

"But you play well. I noticed it in our fresher's party," she added. "And I'm sure the rest of your band members must be equally competitive."

"They are. We do possess some talent. But formulating a band is not as simple as that. It is not an individual performance. And many other aspects are to be taken into consideration." She listened keenly looking straight into my eyes. I moved away mine.

"So we tried hard, but it just did not work." I continued.

"Hmmm." she said, lost in her thoughts.

"Part of life. May be another time. We'll try the next year fest. The worst part is that though I don't have any option right now, but I still want to perform at any cost."

"At any cost, right??" She asked and I said a "Yes."

"Sir, if you don't mind may I suggest something?" I nodded.

"You don't realize but you actually have an option. You can ask for a position in the 'VISHESH'. Who would not like to have a good keyboard player by their side??"

"VISHESH??" I said, trying to hide my grim and wondering at such an idea. In one word, it was irrelevant!

"Yes. But is there something wrong about them??" She had caught me again.

"No."

"You're not meant to hide things. Actually I thought

some of them are your classmates. So it might be helpful. "

"Yeah right. They and help?? Just the way they did a year ago." I tried to wrap up and change the topic. But who could hide things from Ms. Detective. I told her everything.

"So how can I go and ask them now? Tell me." I asked her.

She thought for a while and said, "You said you

Want to perform at any cost. May be a phone call is that cost. You can just let them know that you are interested. Rest is their choice. And we both know getting a positive response can mend everything." She was so unbeatable in pushing someone. After a minute, she received a call.

"Oh no. I did not realize I'm so dead late. I just need to reach for my practice in the mechanical block." She exclaimed the moment she hung up the phone.

"Rescue finally, thank God." I laughed. She pouted.

"I was kidding ma'am. Alright I'll walk you there." I said.

She smiled. Till we both reached the venue, she had given me some more 'convincing' tips. Before she left, she asked me for a final decision if I could call them or not.

"I will but conditions apply." I said.

"And that means."

"That I'll not share my chocolates with you." I said and laughed.

"Not possible. Well, in that case, you can forget about the call." She said teasingly and we laughed harder. I waved her good-bye.

Later that evening, I took fone opened the contact list, found Manav's number and pressed the cancel button. I was totally confused. I wanted to call him up but my ego held me back. It was not that easy for me to forget everything in one flash. But I recalled what Sirat said during the day. After twenty minutes of striving, I managed to press the 'call' button, instead of 'cancel'.

"Hello." it was Manav's voice. I could recognize it since we were friends at some point of time in the pastor at least I thought we were.

"Hii, Aryan here." I said. It's quite hesitant to speak up to someone you never wanted to. A huge chunk of ego needs to be given up for letting that happen.

"Ahh yes. I have your contact number. So, how are you ??" He asked.

"I'm pretty fine. So preparing for the fest??" I could hear the noise behind him, so it was not tough to make out that they were jamming.

"Exactly. You tell me what are you up to?? How come you remember me??"

"Actually, I needed to talk to you about something important."

He listened quietly. Gathering all my courage, I finally spoke up, "Since I knew you guys would be performing,so I thought if I could .... be a part of it. I mean if I can play keyboard with you guys??"

He thought for a while. Unfortunately, conversing over the phone, I could not see his expressions.

"Do you mean with 'VISHESH'??" Of course, I meant 'VISHESH', what else could I be talking about to him.

"Yes, I hope you can help me in this." I said. I could have added 'being a friend of mine' in my statement, but I did not. One of things I hate most is 'Exaggeration'.

"Oh I see. Actually Aryan I need to discuss about this with the rest of the members. I can't promise anything on my own and despair you later." He said.

"Of course. I'll be waiting eagerly." "OK. I'll let you know then."

"By the way, buddy please try and convince them." "I will, for sure. Listen dear, I got to go now." "OK. Bye."

"Bye" he said and hung up the phone.

I felt relieved but at the same time I was tensed too. Relieved because I had solved my dilemma. Tensed because I did not know what the answer would be. I wanted it to be a 'yes' desperately. I could not sleep a wink that night. Dreams of performing in front of the whole college had replaced the slumber in my eyes.

I wanted to call Manav early morning . But I did not want to reveal my nervousness to anyone. I waited till the noon. When the afternoon arrived, I told myself that evening would be a better time.

I called him up at 5:30 pm. He picked up the phone. After a petite chat, I asked him for the answer I was waiting to know.

"You said you people will discuss if I can join you or not." I said.

"Oh yes. I remember. I'm really afraid to say we got too busy last night. The schedule is really very hectic." He said evasively. He did not answer the question that I had asked him.

"So should I understand that you did not disclose the matter to them??"

"No no. I have told them about your esire to join us and we are yet to discuss about it. But you know these busy days. Anyways be patient, Aryan. I'll call you myself this time just as we take a decision." He said consolingly.

"Hmmm. Actually it's only 5 days left for the fest, so I thought if you all could do it at the earliest."

"Yes, yes. I do understand your concern. I'll call you quickly. Do wait for it. " With that, we hung up the phone.

I waited for his call for a couple of minutes. Minutes shortly converted into hours. Somewhere in my heart, I was dreading of getting despaired again.

Next day in the college, I saw Rohit, VISHESH's bass guitarist at some distance. Unlike my usual behaviour, I called out his name the moment he crossed the corridors. He threw a look at me and said mildly, "Yeah."

I signaled him to stop moving and shared with him my wish to be a part of VISHESH. His expression hardly changed when I told him that. So, I asked with hope if Manav had discussed about it with them.

He said in sheer arrogance, "yeah, he was saying something. Aryan, he will tell you more about it." His 'Why-am-I-stuck-here' expression was enough to make me realise that he deserved the kind of behaviour I have shown him in the past year. Expecting anything polite from him was like chasing shadows. Both are a waste of time.

I said, "OK." and left the place.

I wondered if I should call Manav myself. May be I should. After all, I needed them much more than they needed me. But I could not afford to make a fool of myself who stick to someone for their need.

I wish I could meet Sirat somewhere. In my eyes, she seemed much more decisive than me, at least in that matter. But how do I find her?? I did not even have her contact number. That was the first time I wanted to meet her so badly. Sarcastic as life is, I could not see her.

I decided to call up Manav on my own.

"Hello." He spoke.

"Hey." I said thinking what to say next.

"Yeah Aryan, tell me." He said of all possible things I had imagined him saying. How was I supposed to tell him something every time? Had he completely forgotten that he had told me that he'll call me himself?

"Manav actually, the first string of my guitar has broken. I was wondering who I could ask for an extra one. Do you have one??" I asked him.

"I do. You can collect it from me anytime." He said. I expected him to tell me what their final verdict was. He would initiate if they want me to join or at least let me know the other case.

He spoke again, as I was expecting him to. But what he said was a bolt from the blue for me. He said "dude I need to go, they are calling for the practice. Bye. Take care." He hung up the phone the very next second.

I felt like throwing away my phone at the wall. But thanks to Manav. He managed to keep up to my expectations like always. My chances of performing hinged on him, consequently ruined. All over again! I tried hard to test my luck, even till the last days before the fest, but all in vain, fruitlessness. I could not perform on the stage of 2010 fest too.

That year our college had organized a techno-cultural fest. Apart from all the music-dance-and-drama, there were various technical competitions organized for the students.

Pulkit knew that I was upset, so he announced over the phone, "I am putting your name in Virus programming event and we both are going to co-ordinate it." His love for computers and programming had never ceased to gain my attention even before we were friends, the way we are today.

"Man, you are well aware that I don't even have the faintest idea about Virus." I said.

"I know, but I'll make you learn whatever is required and you just need to have a little idea". He said.

"But still. Isn't it a waste of your time?" I said, as I knew clearly that it was an attempt to perk me up.

"It is not, and I'll manage everything. Trust me on that." "OK. Let's go ahead." I said.

I was desperate to get involved and focus on something useful, rather than spending the fest in a grave manner, mourning for another crash attempting for music.

Our team was asked to coordinate a 'Virus programming'

Competition in which the participants were supposed

to code a programs. Though Pulkit taught me some concepts, but making a 'virus' was not my cup of tea.

It hurts only when!!

* * *

On the day of 'Virus programming' competition, I reached college to report on time. But what after that??????

The event began at 10:30 a.m. While the participating teams were trying to make viruses, I was hovering around with my companions keeping an eye on the participants so that no one peeks into the other team's monitor. The labs have been divided so, I had two people with me, Pulkit of course, and Karan, another who was chosen for the task. Both of them were intelligent and were familiar with me.

"Excuse me sir," A team called me. It was not time for teams to wrap up, so I went confidently towards them. I was really certain because I thought they would not have finished the tough task that sooner. "Yeah tell me." I said sounding like a connoisseur of programming.

"Sir we have completed our project, you can check it out." I stayed in awe.

How come so soon? I mean yes, I was not supposed to make silly puzzled expressions glancing at the faces and at their monitor's screen, but to check it. But how could I??

I had never made a virus myself ever. Though I had tried it, but gave up the idea. And how these super intelligent– super confident devils could choose me of all the three? I wondered if they were some distant relatives of Manav. I asked if they were sure. Of course they were. Something clicked in my mind.

"Karan, will you come here, please??" I asked Karan.

Not only intelligent, he was even an obedient down to earth kind of a guy. I asked him to check the query, making an excuse that I had to make a really urgent call. Cell-phones have made life for sure easier. What else does serve as an excuse that works nine out of ten times?

Karan accepted very excitedly as if he was dying to offer his brain some exercise. I came out of the lab as fast as I could, rescuing myself. So when I was out there, enjoying the things around me and wondering what to do, I saw Sirat.

Hush!! This girl meets me at all unexpected times. But days before, when I was praying to see her desperately, it seemed as if she had gone to hibernate in a molehill.

"Oh Hii."

"Hii, Out of breath. Are you going to catch a flight??" she asked. Yes, I was breathing faster since I had just escaped out of the block.

"No no actually, I'm a part of the 'programming team', so pretty occupied with that work."

"Oh I see that really well" she said taunting at me,rolling her eyes.

"You picked me wrong, ma'am. I just came here to get some fresh air." I said, hoping she would believe me.

"Don't worry sir, I won't complain against you." She winked & smiled.

"Hahaha, well that would be so kind of you." I said.

And then I narrated the story of my narrow flee from the geeks who were passionate about making computer virus. She laughed.

"Hey, are you laughing at me? Don't forget I am senior to you." I said, teasing her.

"Hmmm." She said and burst out laughing again. "Tell me. Is there any progress with, VISHESH?"

"I called them that same evening."

"SOOO? What did they say???? " She asked me, light in her eyes reflected, making them shine.

"They fired me, even before the recruitment." I said & laughed. But she did not.

I tried to change the topic. "Don't worry, expecting help from them is next to building a castles in the air. Tell me girl, what is up about your practice?? Announcing this time too ??" I asked her.

"Yeah I'm. And it is going good. After all, it is the only thing I'm doing from years."

"One can guess it easily. You are really good at it." I said. "Ohh, am I??"

"Yes. And I'm not kidding." I said, assuring her.

"Well in that case thanks, sir." She smiled. Her smile-was contagious.

"You're welcome. I think I should go back now, the checking stuff would have got over by now." I said, winking.

She nodded and then said, "Did nobody tell you??" "Tell me what??"

"That you are so mean..." she said, stretching the 'mean' too long.

"Seriously??"

"Yes. So mean..........ingly vivacious." She said, winked at her tactfulness and we both laughed again.

I joined them back, marked my 'present', the reason behind my returning there. Not surprised, Pulkit looked ready to blurt out his frustration for my disappearance amid. But I gave stretched explanations to coax him the very moment we stepped out. We collected the coordinators' certificates the following week.

After the fest, the internal exams took over us as always.

Lectures, labs, some more lectures, and some more labs.

In the second week of April, I received a letter addressing me. It was the re-evaluation result. When I applied for the re-evaluation, I was quite confident. I had a gut feeling that this time I would get a green signal in the 'microprocessors and interface' exam. Though none of my wishes got processed at all and I hinged on the interface of failure again. I did not clear this time too. May be, it would take me some more time to get rid of this stain on my mark-sheet, I thought to myself.

Meanwhile all this, my interaction with Sirat inflated. And she became a friend, a friend who had all the stupid qualities in this world that a human being can possess.

We exchanged contact numbers purely for academic reasons. She said that she wanted to ask for some queries regarding one of the subjects.

"Don't worry. I would not bother you by giving blank calls day and night." She tried to assure me and made fun at the same time.

"That does not seem possible as far as I know you." I teased her back.

But she did not step back from her words and asked me only about study-related things over the text. Sometimes, I would drop a forwarded message in her inbox. She too started doing the same. She called me once to wish Good day. Quite unsurprisingly, we kept talking and talking and hung the phone after twenty seven minutes.

Semester exams approached. I knew I had one more thing to accomplish- the 'microprocessor' exam. How difficult it seems to study the same book all over again for clearing a backlog. But I could not afford to take a chance this time. So I chose to study it hard. All the exams went off well. Yes, all of them.

Sitting with juniors during the Microprocessor's exam, it felt really awkward. And, I tried ignoring whenever any known junior came around me. However since, there were many of my classmates, the embarrassment decreased gradually. And thank God, it went nice.

The semester was done, so now it was time for the third year training. My rendezvous with Chandigarh had taught me an indispensable lesson that there's no place like home. Staying at home and working on your own can be much more improvising than roaming motiveless in institutions. So I decided to take up the training in Kurukshetra itself, which meant I could traverse down there for one hour and come back just after the class. It helped me a lot in utilizing my time for music properly. And to be honest, I was much more devoted towards my training than I was the last time. I can proudly say that I made those 45 days quite productive in real sense.

We joined college on 15th September. The fourth year had begun, the final year of my engineering. The past three years had taught me enough to play cool by now. I did not drag things when chucking them off was easy. I began to enjoy the pleasure of sitting on back benches, quite contrary to my favourite spot in the first two years of my engineering, the front rows.

I was trying hard to make guitar a charm of my hands. Fortunately, I had succeeded in getting familiar with the six strings. So, I could hold my head high and announce to myself that MUSIC was in action. There was one thing more that demanded equal attention from me was my job placement. I was in the final year and at this stage not paying any heed to recruitment could be the best way to bully one-self. So I made up my mind to concentrate on it all along, even though it was four months away.

Somehow, it became habitual for me to talk to the

'kiddish' girl, as I used to call her teasingly. Meanwhile, many people, who I bothered about or not were busy pondering over my craving to form a music band. Uninvited criticism was a gift that I was endowed with, that too in abundance. It did not hurt me. Dogs bark any way. Those lampoons wanted me to give up, but I did not.

But what affected me was when my best friend Pulkit ended up saying one day, "You still want to do this??"

"I did not get what you mean."

He thought for a while and then spoke the most unpleasant line he could ever say, "The music band andall, yaar. Look Aryan, you've wasted considerable amount of your time and hardly earned anything till now."

My world blacked out on hearing it from his mouth, as he continued "And what if you even succeed now, it's the last year Aryan, no one would remember that you ever made a band."

I kept quiet. May be he took my silence as my resignation. I did not get infuriate at him because his concern for me was making him speak the pits. But I was hurt and disappointed. What about my EGO!! What I knew was just that I was in no state to step back. Doing that is no less than insanity, especially when you have set your heart on that thing for that long.

I wanted to talk to someone, somebody who would not be as dishearted as everybody else. During this time, Sirat and I started exchanging messages. She would often send me something answerable. 'Choose one and I'll tell you' this kind of stuff and we would start chatting.

I called up Sirat for the first time myself. "Hello." She said as she picked up the phone. "Hello." I tried to sound normal.

"Hi how are you?"

"I'm pretty good, you tell me, how are you?" "Sir, I'm

confused."

"Confused regarding what??"

"That should I propose to you or not." She said and burst out laughing.

I wondered if that was a joke.

"Whatever." I said. But she clarified herself saying she was kidding.

"Actually, I'm confused about the reason that is making you sound so low??"

"Really? Do I?"

"Of course you are. And your victorious 'Do-I' is not working this time. You can tell me what is it?"

I was quite again, which was enough for her to realize that it was not the right moment. It was not that I did not want to tell her. But the question was how??

She flipped on to something else. "So tell me something what is happening around?"

"I'm just at home. Waiting for my dinner, mum is cooking may be." I said half-heartedly.

"Wow, you made me skip a beat. I mean home and the food."

"Hmmm. So, do you miss your home??"

"A LOT..! I mean more than anything else. In fact, I was just planning to go back home the upcoming weekend. But two days would not be enough. I would kill most of the time on the way itself. " She sounded disappointed, of course a way less disappointed than I was.

"Hmmm. So where do you belong to?" I asked her, not to run out of the conversation.

"Delhi. And by the way, you don't even know this." She questioned complaining the very next moment.

"I'm sorry. I did not know the mental asylum got shifted from Agra to Delhi. Otherwise, I would not have asked this. By the way, when did it shift? " I laughed harder. So did she..

"Ohh so Delhi girl, hmm. That makes me think I should stay away from you. I have heard they are a real trap." I continued teasing.

"Real trap? Huh, as if you're that naive!"

Finally I told her about the non-gracious comments that I got to listen. She listened very patiently when I told her all this. There was something nice about her. She knew when not to crack jokes.

After talking to her, there was one thing clear in my mind. Criticism by your closest ones can be of great use sometimes. You may hate them for the critics at that moment but it can make you spurs on heights, more than anything else. I wanted to make my desire come alive. I knew I had to pull up my socks for this. It was the last chance for me to prove I was right, and others were not.

I was confident this year that I could manage to play guitar on the stage now. Moreover I was pushed to try harder than even before. So, I was determined to get us all together again. I did not know whom to start with. I was a bit subtle to call Arpit. But I had to, since he was a necessity for the band, plus he would require much more time to pick up than the rest of us. I was aware of this in my hearts of hearts. I called him up.

"Hello." He said. "Hello."

How are you??"

"I am fine dude. I was just thinking about you."

"About me? Hey wait wait, man I am not that way." I said and laughed at him.

"Shut up man, neither am I. And you dare not suspect about it. Actually, I was thinking about the fest. Our performance."

"The music band??" I asked him.

"That's it. I think we should reunite and try again if you agree." He said. Oh God, was he reading my mind so that he could say all this?

"Agree??"

He interrupted before I could say anything and said "yes.

And I have made up some balance too for paying you back the cost of the drums, like we discussed before. May I buy them from you??"

I felt like jumping on the sofa I was sitting on.

"Yeah. But are you sure that you want to?"

"Hmmm, I'm. But you are the pivot, man. Don't say no."

"No?? Dear, I swear I just called you to ask about our take on the reunion and you just stole my words. That's so unbelievable." I told him.

I sold him the drums for Rs. 3500. The loss of a few hundred made me earn an invaluable profit. He looked so sure and interested unlike the last time. I made him promise that he'll practice them from then onwards.

Once I had to go to college at seven in the evening to borrow a book from a friend of mine. I was passing through the corridor of boys' hostel when I saw three to four guys practicing with their instruments. It is 'VISHESH', so I try not to go close and maintain a distance from them.

Suddenly, my gaze fell on one of those guys and I took a step back. It is tough to understand his presence there. He is neither Manav, nor Rohit. He is Jatin. But, was he not on my side?

Yes, he was but only till the moment I saw him with them. On my way back to home, I realize what could make him turn his back at us. I understood why he has been in a 'no-message-no-call' genre from so many days. Of course why would he need to acknowledge me now, realizing I am of least benefit to him.

'VISHESH' required a guitarist we heard from the starting days of 7th semester, ever since Tushar, Vishal and

Sandy had completed their degree and bid adieu to the college and their band,their requirement must have got fulfilled in form of Jatin. Of course like others, he too has deemed that we would never succeed. And accepting him would have overjoyed Manav and Rohit, because it will pinch me to lose him. I decide to consider Jatin a bygone from then. It was also the day when I took the stand of buying an electric guitar.

After the internal exams, one day I meta guy with typical blonde hair. Someone we don't usually find in a place like ours. He came up to me and shook hand. My confused expression spoke for me and I asked, "Do I know you??" My memory had never been amy good friend.

"Sir, I am Ajit, you did not recognize me."

I tried hard to recognise, but I could not. All that I could make up was that I had seen this face earlier.

"Sir, you auditioned for a vocalist last year." I nodded. "I was one amongst the guys. I did a rap." He said, finally helping my 'tube-light' brain to glow up.

"Oh yeah. I remember. I'm really sorry. "

"Oh c'mon sir. It's ok. I wanted to know if you are forming a band this time."

Tough question to answer. Of course, I wanted to, but the only doubt was... Actually everything, except my will, was a big question mark for me.

"Yeah. We'll try again I suppose. We will." I articulated hoping each word of my statement comes true.

"Sir, if you don't mind may I ask something?" "Go ahead." I smiled at him.

"Actually I was thinking if I could try and join your band. I have even brought an electric guitar and I'm trying to learn it by following video tutorials over the internet." He said to my utmost surprise pushing me into a world of thoughts.

"That seems interesting I said. So, how long has it been that you are trying this way??" I asked him.

"Around 10 weeks and I can do chord-shifting easily." He answered confidently.

Before I could say something, he said, "Sir, I'm quite awake to the fact that how much you are pining to do some music action on the fest stage. Just like you, I too have that desire."

There was zeal in his voice when he said that. I made a decision in my mind, but his words made me assure that I was doing the right thing.

I went back and recalled that he had done a good job in rapping. But the reason why we did not choose him was it was our first chance to perform. And I could not afford to gamble on it, so we'd decided to play safe. But now, a year after, my belief in conventionality had evaporated in the air. Life is all about risks. And who knows, he may turn out to be the knight in shining armour.

"Ok. I think we can consider atleast thinking about you as a part of the band. "

"So does that mean…??" He asked impatiently.

"Yes, but I can judge only after a trial. Would you mind that?"

"Of course not." He agreed whole-heartedly.

I knew that he was a good rapper. It was something that one could easily make out. His extra-fair skin and that sort of hair were backlog to his talent. I just wanted to get assured about his guitar playing abilities.

We went to his hostel room, during the lunch the very next day. I asked him to play the rhythm and do some chord shifting. To my surprise, he played quite well, though there wasa lot of room for improvement. But that's the way you learn. He had even bought an amplifier and aprocessor along with his electric guitar. So in my mind, I was determining the pros and cons of inviting him in the band. Certainly, the pros outweighed the cons.

He also introduced me to his roommate, Anshul.

"Sir, Anshul also has interest in playing guitar." Ajit told me.

"Ohh that is really nice. So can you also play like Ajit,??" I asked him.

"Not that good, sir. He is all into music. However, I do it just for my enjoyment. But yes, it inspires me a lot of times. Actually when Ajit announced that he was going to buy an electric guitar, I was at the top of excitement."Anshul said.

"Hehe. Yeah. That even makes me remember many things." Lunch got over and we all had to come back.

"Sir, what have you decided about me?" Ajit asked me, while we were all marching out of the boys hostel.

"I think I will be certifiable to invite you to perform with us." I said to him mentioning the date October 28th, 2010.

I was aware of what had ruined my plans and crushed my hopes in the previous year. So I wanted to start the practice sessions as soon as possible this time, so that we have plenty of time to fall in perfect synchronization with each other.

Ajit and I started playing together. I gave a thought to involve Arpit too from day one, but then it would be a blunder to repeat the same mistake all over again. I did not want too many cooks to spoil the broth that I was waiting for, for years. So I thought patiently and practically.

As we started this time, I felt the same as I did a year ago. Some things never fail to make an ignition inside you. These are actually one's true passion. But this time it was a 'do or die' situation for me. When I got tired and wanted to call off practice, I would tell myself "If not this year, it would never again be. Never Ever!" And suddenly a force would push me back again.

I received a text that evening saying the fourth semester's result was out. The very next moment I switched on my PC and logged onto the university's website. Typing my roll number took me back to the memoirs of the past the last time. I wished today was not going to be like that scary one. As the request was being processed, different questions continued to dart inside me. The questions my pounding heart was again questioning my brain.

What if I flunk this time again?? What if I had to pay for somebody else's mistake?? What if this result too proves out to be an envoy of disappointment??

As the required webpage opened up, I gathered enough courage and read what it said. It said that I had cleared all papers. Thank God. He had finally done justice to me, by not letting me down. The subject called, Microprocessor & Interface was no longer a hurdle in my way. I could finally sit in any interview.

A week later, I got my revised mark sheet from the university, the one without any stains. I had scored 66 marks in M.I. It brought an equally broad smile on my face as the first semesters did. Of course, the thing valued the most is always the one that you have waited for the longest. With this mark sheet, my folder of document got completed.

I was practicing along with Ajit when his cell phone beeped. He went back to check the message.

"Oh crap." He said the next moment, making me wonder what made him react like that.

"what's wrong ??" I asked him.

"I suppose." He said and passed over his cell phone to me.

There was a message from Anshul which said:

"Date sheet over the net. Finals commence next Monday."

I was taken aback. I managed to ask him "Are you sure he is not trying to befool??"

"Sir, he is not that kind of a guy."

The next moment, Pulkit called me up, finally clearing

all our doubts. "Yes I've checked it on the internet myself."

"That is no way man. I had so many hopes about our practice." I was pissed off.

"Hmm. Any ways where are you??" I told him I was at the practice. Obviously, he did not appreciate but kept mum in order not to contribute my already spoiled mood.

"Ok, let's see."

I said and disconnected the phone. And soon to my wildest hopes, the exams appeared up in front of us out of nowhere.

When destiny plays its role!

* * *

Least to say, we had to put our practice in abeyance. It was not a decision but a imposition that we were forced to follow. I gave a thought about how to carry on our practice sessions for some days, but they were of no avail. After all, I could not afford to score a crash in the 4th year of my engineering.

The finals went really well. To me, the four subject's course looked like a child's play after having to study the six-plus-one subjects, last year. Finally to my resort, my last exam got finished on 6th Jan 2011. I was a man of my own wishes again, untamed.

It was almost a week after the new year, 2011's arrival bought me a good news. So now there were no exams, no backlog, luckily. And it was time for me to get in order for recruitment. Our college usually brings 'Tata Consultancy Services' or better known as TCS in the first week of

February. So I realized that I had to pull up my socks

and secure a job for myself, so that I do not have to get out of this college taking home the tag of being 'idle and jobless'.

My exams had got over soon as I had just four subjects in the semester, but for Sirat, it was many yards to go. Her exams were meant to wrap up after 10 days.

From the day I knew the fact that she was good in English, we always conversed in English and I asked her to spot grammatical errors in my language. I had also asked her once if she would help me out during my placement drills and she promised she would, at any cost and she fulfilled when the time came.

She was a good student and had secured a presentable mark sheet for herself. So even though, I was quite confident about her performance in her own exams, still I did not want her to ruin her degree.

We were coming out of the Computers department she mocked, "Are you writing depressing poetry these days??"

"Yes. How did you figure this out?" I mocked back. "Your serious thoughtful expression told that to me."

"Actually, I'm thinking about something important." I said to her and added as an afterthought, "It is nice that you are still determined to assist me, but you should not avoid the fact that you still have some exams left, I mean." "Sir, so you want to convey that I should behave mean, and step back from my own words. And say 'Good luck' to you?" she retorted.

"No no, see if you do not get good marks, you would come and blame me in the end, won't you??"

"Oh, I will surely." She tittered and then said, "I have an idea. Let's say I have exams so I'll study like my routine, and after finishing my target, when I go to bed, I'll talk to you at that time. What do you say?"

I was confused to the depth, as always.

"See, I'm not sacrificing studies, but just giving up a bit of sleep. So it can work." She said.

"I can and that's quite thoughtful of you, ma'am."

"Thanks. Ok, tell me something important, you have less than a month in hand. How are you going to prepare?? "

"I have laid a schedule for it. I'll start with the 7th semester's syllabus, since it is quite afresh in my mind, and then I'll take up the sixth semester's course, and the rest will follow one after the other. "

"That sounds like your road to success. And what about me??"

"I'm counting on you Sirat, and you are so selfish, huh! This was not what I expected from you." I told her dramatically.

I could see her expressions changing abruptly. She must have been wondering what she did so wrong in a split second. And then I added, "You have one complete year to go for your placements. Mine is just a month away and you are worried about yourself asking 'What about me?'" with that, I burst out laughing at the top of my lungs.

"Oh my goodness! You are just gone." She said and mocked hitting me with the book in her hand. But then managing to control my laughter, she got back, "I just wanted to know how can I help you in this?"

"Yeah, you can help." I told her absent- mindedly. "That is what I'm asking. In what way??"

"I have thought about this too. Look you can help in preparing tricky questions from the course of your present semester. "

"Ohh! So, that is some kind of a mock interview."

Thank God, she understood.

"Exactly. And you know what! It can prove out to be a really good exercise." I told her as a matter-of-fact.

She nodded and asked, "Are you sure I can lend a hand??"

"Of course, but only if Ms. Interviewer knows something to ask." I ridiculed.

"And of course if Mr. Interviewee promises to give her a treat after he gets placed." She chuckled. We both smiled because both of us were waiting for it to happen.

My preparations for "TCS" began on 10th Jan-2011. I had talked to many seniors who got placed there and had gathered enough information which could serve as a great aid for me to differentiate between what to do and what not to. They had even given me some tips regarding their recruitment policy. So now the mist from my eyes evaporated making me see my target clearly.

Level 1~ the multiple choice questions test.

To prepare for the first round of my ordeal, I had brought the aptitude books. It looked like a volcano of interrogations ready to erupt any moment taking me in its gulp. During the day, I would study and revise the course so that nights could be employed for revisions and doubts.

It was not that much easy to get placement in TCS. I didn't want to take any chance. So mugging up from just a book was not really satisfactory. I had decided to crack the kind of questions that appeared from time to time.. I had downloaded them from the internet. Of course, internet can serve more than just being a time-killer. There is no essence like 'internet', when put into good use. Who else could make it sound better than a potential computer engineer himself?

Though we decided to study on our own, but Pulkit and I had settled to meet once after every week to discuss each other'sdoubts. We were at my place when we wrapped up with the queries and were enjoying tea.

He said "you know Manav called me two days ago."
"Did he??" I was amazed.

"Indeed. He wanted to talk about you." Now it was another time I was knocked for a six yet again.

"About me? Ahh, great!! Good going, buddy. As much as I'm enjoying this prank, chuck it." I told him, dismissing his ridiculous sense of humour.

"I'm damn serious. It is not a hoax." He said believingly.

"Ok. So what did he say??"

"He said that he wanted your help. So he wanted me to put that picture before you. "

"Of course, why would he call us with any interest of his own? Manav was so predictable."

"Yeah, he had some university chores pending and your acquaintance who works there can help."

"Ohoho. So who do I look like?? Mother Teresa??"I said.

"Hehe. To him, may be you do." He giggled.

"Any way, what did you tell him?" I enquired.

"That I'll try if I get to speak to you. So you can call him."

My eyes widened up. I told him back "Why should I call him? If he needs, he'll call me on his own."

"I am surviving on the hope that he does. It would be fun." he said.

"We are gossiping now, you know." I alarmed him.

Of course, after a hiatus of time, every discussion befalls into the category of gossips.

"May be, but you better tell me the moment he calls you."

He said.

I wondered how Pulkit could be that sure that he will.

I was busy, tormenting myself with another dose of never-ending and mind-wrecking questions when I received a call.

Without even looking at the caller's name, I answered the the call "Hello." Must be Pulkit or Sirat, I thought to myself.

"Hii, Manav here." He was too mild to be heard properly. "Pardon." I said, as I checked for the name on my phone's screen.

"Manav, your classmate." I was astounded. Poor Manav must have been tough for a Guitarist in the college's most popular band to prove his identity.

"Ohh I'm sorry. I was just occupied."

"It's ok. So tell me how come you called??" I said enacting as if I was too naive to know anything.

"Hmm. So I suppose, Pulkit did not get to tell you anything about me."

"Pulkit????" I said as if I had heard this name for the first time.

"Ok." He took a deep breath and then spoke, "Aryan, buddy I want your help. Actually there are some errors in my mark sheet so I had sent it back to the University for making corrections. But they are behaving really evasively. "

"Hmmm, ok. So, what am I I'm supposed to do??"

"I heard that an uncle of yours works there at a high post. So things can become easier if you talk to him on my behalf."

"Ohhh. So that is the situation."

"Aryan, I suppose you'll help me, being a friend" He said. "Friend", now that word sounds too fake from his mouth.

"Of course, but see Manav, I can't talk to my uncle directly. But I can try asking dad to do that."

"Okk. But please do it *yaar*, it is really important for me. And if you can help..." He mumbled for a minute longer and then we hung up the phone. In my mind, his words resonated again and again "if you can help", yeah, that is what you heard me say Mr. Manav, a year ago. Remember the way you treated me then.

How amazing it is, with the passage of time, situations and circumstances remain same, but people swap positions. Back then I was pleading in front of a guy for an opportunity, but he shoved me away. After a lapse of 365 days, time was taking its toll. He was right there doing the same. And I was clear about the way, he deserves to get treated.

At a moment, I wished I would go and talk to dad about helping him. But my ego, the rage in my mind stopped me from doing that.

For now, I had managed to bring my third and fourth semester's course to closing moments. And Sirat's exams were about to finish too. Only one paper was left, so she took a sigh of relief. She had declared it herself 'in your services, highness. Just order me'. How could this girl preclude herself from the offence of not helping the divine?" It all went over my head. God, she was so filmy.

"That is sooo cheesy. But I can make out that your exam went well."

"Certainly. Finally, I'm out of the cage. "

"Not yet. There is one more to go." I brought her back to the reality.

"Yeah, but that's after 7 long days. I'll worry about it when I am2-3 days close."

"That is what they call 'true engineering'. So tell me, are you ready with the questions**?"**

"Yes, so here we go without any jokes." "Exactly!"

"And sir, you won't make me laugh." "Sirat, do I sound like a clown??"

"Tough question! Ok so sorry. But at least for the next 10 questions, nobody plays the kid, right?"

"That would be hard for you, ma'am. Now shall we, please??" I asked, pleading her.

"Ok so question 1......"

I answered eight out of the first ten questions correctly. Not only questioning, she even appreciated when I gave the right answer. It helped me hike my confidence level too.

We kept doing this intriguing exercise for the next hour. We discussed the questions or precisely she told me the things that I could not answer. Honestly, she did it so sincerely, that I did not feel shy or embarrassed to learn from a junior. Instead, I was willing to learn more. It was quite apparent that she too had worked on it.

"Thanks a lot for helping me." I told as we completed with the interrogation.

"You need not say this. Don't worry. I'm not doing it for you." she said.

"Then who are you doing it for??

TCS! So that they get a pearl like me..!" I smirked at her.

"How modest. Well, I'm doing it for myself." "Like what??"

"Like, for the treat that you would owe me." "Treat?? Which treat??" I said and we both laughed.

Two days later, Manav called me again. "Hello." I picked up the phone.

"Hello. Aryan, how are you??" "I'm pretty fine. You tell me??"

"I'm screwed up buddy." Finally the scoundrel admitted the truth. He added, "I told you about it two days ago."

"Yeah that's a real sort of mess." I tried to sympathize with my "dear friend".

"Hmmm. Did you talk to your dad about it??" I was thinking hard to knit a story. "Yes. I did"

"Oh good, so he must have talked to your uncle. What did he say??" I kept quiet. At least give me a second, dude.

"Unfortunately no, actually dad tried but his family told that he had gone to Hyderabad for an educational conference."

"Ohh shit." He sounded disappointed. "Buddy, will you ask your dad to talk to him once more? Just once, please."

"I'll do that and let you know what happens."

"Ok, please try it soon. I fear I would not be allowed to qualify for TCS if I don't get it shortly."

"Hmm. I understand. Don't worry, I'll see to it."

"I'll call you soon. Please don't let my hopes down".

"Yes. I'll call you just as I get to know something. I have some urgent work. Bye."

"Ok bye-bye." I hung the phone and went back to pour my attention on what was actually important to me, my preparations.

The first job interview is one of the things in life one can rarely forget. As I looked up in the mirror after dressing up in formal white shirt and black trousers, mixed feelings sprinted in me. It was going to be DIFFERENT that day. After all, it was the day when my fate could decide, even if it was for a couple of upcoming years. I had been making careful preparations for it and no matter what, I had to make them count. Though my family was equally excited and a bit nervous as I was, I was given a confidence and enough boost before I left home for the placement drill.

The level 1 begin at 10 a.m. sharp and was a test confined to aptitude questions. Even though it was not really tough, but I found most of my classmates, even those who were far better scorers than me, exaggeratingly cribbing and panicking. The results were out as the clock tick 2

O"clock. And I was in!

So what stood firm in front of me were the interviews, the real job! From day 1, I had been exposed to the fact that I don't look studious. I had worn anti glares to look somewhat intelligent.

Level 2~ The technical Interview Round

It had to be harder. And it demanded a lot more than just technical facts and concepts scrumming in your head. It needed confidence, and placidity. Even if I knew 100 things, and I was not able to convey even one of them, it would mean assured failure. Though I was playing cool from the morning, nervousness was still building up. Thankfully, I was called for the interview before it overtook me completely.

In the interview room, everything depends on the way you answer the first question put up. For me, it was a soar. After one or two questions the interviewer asked me something Sirat had put upon me in the mock-interviews. And though I was not sure when I gave its answer to her, but today I was hell as confident about it. As the interview proceeded, I succeeded in making a good impression. Their expressions made it evident. They liked pedantic stuff I guess.

Just as I walked out of the room, I texted Sirat and told it to her and that my interview went nice.

"Your resume speaks that you are a sheer believer of optimism, how??" The petite lady sitting in front of me, asked. To make it clear, she was the H.R. executive of the recruitment team of the awaited TCS.

And if you are confused, guessing my existence in front of her, I would remove all your doubts that I had reached the final level of interview,- the H.R. interview. And this prestigious moment of sitting in front of her had come in my luck after succeeding in first two levels and slogging for past fifteen hours.

I nodded in order to acknowledge her question when she spoke. The first thing that came to my mind was MUSIC.

I told her briefly about how I was attempting to make a music band from two and half years, subsequent failures did not stop me and I was not willing to give up yet.

"That's quite impressive." She said. Definitely, I was about to reach cloud nine on hearing that. But she brought me back the next second by adding "But many people can take it as a form of stubbornness."

"It is a matter of perception. But yes, I do feel that good end results can shut mouths better than good arguments.

Ma'am, I suppose you'll agree to this." I did not mind using sugarcoating techniques, if they earn me a job, which pays 30,000 bucks per month. But then who would?

"Undoubtedly I do. So, I'm done with the questions. We'll let you know the rest very shortly."

"Sure. Thanks ma'am." She smiled.

After my interview, I was confident. It had gone well for me and I stood a good chance, at least I assumed it to be.

12 February 2011, 6:10 p.m.

I was wandering with my brother Ishu in our farms, when I checked my mailbox. There was a new mail,the most valued and auspicious one for my career. It was from TCS.

I had got selected. My hard work had been rewarded by God. Overjoyed, I was at the top of cloud nine. Perhaps, I was not panicking like my classmates, but my happiness certainly had no limits. The next moment, I received a call from Pulkit and he told me that he too received the mail. Something I expected considering his abilities! I was curious to know who else had got placed amongst my classmates. And then Pulkit told me Manav, Rohit, Tanya have made it to TCS too. Long sigh!!!!

I wondered someone would have helped Manav. But I was happy for myself. We went back home to announce my achievement. Mom and dad were happy, proud, touched and everything they could be. The next moment, dad asked us to bring sweets. Indeed, it was time for celebrations for them. For now, I had secured a job, celebrated. I had eradicated the spot on my degree, thankfully. My command over english had improved and was still improving. Music, the best things always take the longest time!!

The fest was around, so getting a room allotted for practicing was not a tough job. The only tough part was making it useful. We started jamming together on 2nd March 2011. Our search for the bass guitarist had found solace in Anshul, Ajit's roommate. He was a polite and ajovial guy, who met all our requirements. He was not that skilled, but his curiosity for playing guitar was immovable. That is all what we expected from him. He followed what we asked him to do. He took no time in buying a bass guitar. Though he was a novice with the instrument, he was a fast learner which made my job easier. I heard Arpit playing the drums. It reflected that he had worked on it since he played way better than the last time.

With the amps and pedals, we got solutions to many of the problems we faced. We had finally reached a stagewhere we could decide a song to play.

"Will you be able to sing Hindi songs?" I asked Ajit. I feltridiculed at the same question I posed at him. He made a sore expression like the one a drawing teacher makes, when he is asked to perform karaoke.

"I can't really say. I can, but it would be difficult to bona fide it as 'singing.'"

I was wondering about what to say next, but then he added "I'm really comfortable at singing some english songs, yes." He looked really confident. I nodded.

"Ok, Thumbs up to that. It would be good if you can hymn anything in our native language, we need that." I said as I realized that he was waiting for my affirmation.

"Aryan is right. It is what actually makes the crowd rise to ecstasy." Arpit said, as we both looked at the Ajit with eyes full of expectations.

"I can do a Punjabi rap. What do you have to say about that??" he said, after thinking for a while.

"That would be awesome..!!" I said. Yes, it would be thrilling.

Luckily, Arpit also gave a positive reaction. After all, I was craving day and night to formulate a band which is different from others. And the only possible way was playing out-of-the-box music.

"So, what we want now is some nice popular English songs and rap. Audiences always enjoy what they have heard at least once." I told them.

Though it turned a debate picking a song, we finally agreed to settle with **a song** of Linkin Park and one rap by Honey singh. We started practicing the songs with enthusiasm. Things were going well, but somehow something seemed incomplete. When I shared this with my band, they got what I wanted to convey.

"Yes, I agree we desire another vocalist too. I think we can call Sameer." He said as matter-of-fact.

"No. We actually desire a female vocalist." I suggested.

"Female vocalist?" The three of them asked in unison. I had been expecting this.

"See, we want make our band's performance to be memorable, right??"

"yessss!!." They all nodded.

"We have a rapper, who is quite promising enough. Alls good with that. But at the end of the day, we cannot ignore the fact that conventional music is the forte of a music band. "

"Yeah that is understandable, but why specifically, a female singer only??" Ajit asked.

"Because nobody can haunt the audiences, as a girl can."

Arpit spoke and smiled to me. His line made me remind Sirat. I wondered if he was a making a dig at me. Of course, that was my part of imagination, since nobody amongst them knew Sirat.

We had put a notice on the notice-board stating our requirements for a female singer.

In the evening, I received a call from Sameer. What would I tell him now, I asked my brain. Pick up the phone first, you idiot, it replied back.

"Hello."

"Hello, sir." After a bit of conversation, he asked me "sir, I've heard you are making a band."

I had to tell him someday, I knew. "You have heard it right. Sameer, look yaar, I really wanted to involve you this time. But situations changed on my part."

"Hmmm. I guess."

"But please don't take me wrong."

"It's ok, sir. I can understand. And it's completely your choice." His words made me feel relieved.

"Yeah so tell me, what are you doing on the fest? Do we expect a solo performance?" I asked.

"Not solo. But yes, I'm making a music band this time." I was shocked.

"A band, How come so soon??"

"I have found a fresher who plays drums really well and a friend of mine who has agreed to give the bass. And I can play the rhythm, sir. " he took pride in telling me that.

"Oh really??."

"Yeah, but we are trying hard, so let see.

Sir I wanted to ask you something as well."

"Go ahead."

"I wanted to ask you if you'll be playing the lead from our side or we can collaborate with you guys"

"You mean as the lead guitarist?"

"No no, we leave it up to your convenience. Be it through keyboard, or guitar." He tried to convince me, for a couple of minutes.

"Sameer, you have always been nice to me. I do respect it. But I'm sorry. I can't join your band. I have already promised three guys, and I can't go back on my words, at the end moment." I denied his offer. There was one morereason behind it. I was not confident about them. I could not take the risk to believe in a band the just constructed overnight.

But before we hung up, he said one thing "but I was craving to perform with someone experienced, you, it would have done a world of good to us."

The next day, our hunt for a female voice began, but that was not the only qualification we were looking for. Of course, we could not mention it in the notice, but I had borne in my mind that the 'girl-to-be-bestowed' must possess striking looks. After all, looks did matter at least here.

Through auditions, we finally found a girl who satisfied the necessities of our band. Her name was Payal. She sang quite ok if not great, but she was the most prominent looking amongst all others who had shown up at the audition.

Taking into consideration her voice quality, we had selected two popular songs for Payal to sing. It took a little time for her but yes, she was giving her best not to let us down. The preparations for the fest had commenced in the college. So that meant no classes, full day practice, and lots and lots of disturbances by the people hovering around, aimlessly.

Who would not like to be surrounded by audiences, but certainly not in the practice sessions!! Especially if the spectators scream every time your singer began to sing. "All check??" I asked them, while the five of us were practicing for the performance in the practice room. They nodded.

"So here we all go for the ride." Ajit sang his part, and it was Payal's turn. She started off well but one ofthe lines in her song had an equivocal meaning. When she sang it, the 'external factors' made a very loud roar. She looked really uncomfortable and remained quite. Her reaction was quite expected.

"Don't worry. Ignore them." I said, trying to raise her spirits.

"Hmm. You can continue." Ajit said. After a couple of seconds, Payal regained some confidence and started singing again. That had become a routine of practice for us.

One day while she was reharsing , few boys from outside passed really terrible comments which made her heart sink. That day, our comforting words and jokes could not manage to soothe her up. Amidst the practice, she left the practice room saying she needed a break'.

"Heya." I said as I saw her returning back to the practice room the next day.

"Hiii." She said looking bothered. But I did not ask her about it, thinking it might not be comfortable for her to talk about the previous day.

"So, early today??" I asked her, breaking the awkward silence.

"But we don't even have a complete week left in our hands."

"Do we have another option than trying??" of course, we could not waste more time in crying over the spilt milk.

In the core of my heart, I knew it would not be impossible to find another vocalist since many girls had appeared on the auditions. We had started our quest again and luckily we were getting results. We were hopeful that in a day or two, we would get an apt girl.

Meanwhile we were benefited unknowingly. News travel fast making Payal realise that she was missing out on something people generally crave for. She could see that our loss of a vocalist was now transforming in to her own loss.

While I was practicing with my mates, she called me up. I came out of the room and I answered her call.

"Hello."

"Hello, sir. Please don't disconnect the phone." She said hurriedly assuming that I was going to do so. If I would have to disconnect, why would I have bothered picking up anyways. I did not speak, but stayed on the line, waiting for her to say that she had called up for.

"Sir, I wanted to talk to you about something." Now, this line had begun to frighten me. Usually, people tend to use it as an introducing weapon to all the tortures.

"What is it?" I said in a no-nonsense tone.

"Sir, I'm really very sorry about that absurd bhaviour of mine. I realize that it should not have been done." She apologized.

"It is good for you to know that. Anything else you want to say, or... " ok, maybe, I was getting too rude, but that is what she was ought to get.

"Yes, sir. I wanted to ask if...." she was finding hard to say what she wanted to. But I was in no mood to mollify her nervousness. And then she gave me another jolt.

"Sir, may I re-join your band please??" "Come again. What did you just say??"

"Sir, I have realized in the past one and a half day, that I've thrown an axe on my own feet by saying 'no', and I do regret it but ...." she mumbled for some more minutes.

"Sir, can you please say something now??" She asked me in a pleading tone.

"I can't sit in the ivory tower and judge, whether you should be allowed to come back. We'll discuss about it and tell you." I hung up the phone, saying this.

"Payal called just now." I came back in the practice room and told them.

Three of them threw confused looks at me only till Arpit gave voice to their thoughts.

"What did she say??"

"She wants to make a comeback in our band." "Really?? She said all this by herself." Ajit asked me.

I nodded. He looked relieved. "So, we should bring her back. What did you tell her??"

"Wait a second, Ajit." Arpit told him and turned his eyes to me.

"What is your take, Arpit??" I asked him.

Perplexed, he shrugged. Ajit raised his eyebrows.

Arpit said, "I can't say, man. She walks out of the situation any time, and rings up to apologize for it, the next day. Is this a hoax??"

"Exactly. It would not be that easy for us."

"But do you think she is willing enough this time??" "She does sound convincing. So, let us just consider it." "But.... " he protested a little"Look dear, I understand that what she did was completely wrong, but we need to think rationally. We practically have just 4 days left. Of course, it would be difficult for us to adjust with her now, but it'll be far easier than finding a new girl and guide her. Isn't it??"

"It is, for sure." And then no more interrogations were made by Arpit."

Payal called me half an hour later. "Sir, what have you guys decided and have you made up your mind??"

"See, Payal it's not easy for us."

"So does that means...." disappointed, she stopped without completing her sentence.

"That means it involved a stretched discussion. You are invited back, only if..."

"Only if??"

"You take it meaningfully."

"I would, sir. I promise, and things would not repeat."

"There's one more thing."

"Yes sir??"

"Ya, reach the practice room tomorrow sharp at 9 a.m."

So finally things returned back on the track. I crossed fingers till the final moment. The moment had come when we were asked to get our band's name registered for performance in the BATTLE OF BANDS.

"But we have not decided the name yet." Arpit said.

"Hardly matters buddy, we'll do it now." I said.

"Sir, what should be like?? Music??"

"Maybe or may be related to us??" Arpit said. "Boys of beat.", Said Ajit.

"Sorry, dear. But Yuck!!!" Anshul said as we laughed.

"Never mind. By the way, there's something common

between the 4 of us." I said

"Let me say, the first letter of our name. They all begin with 'A'. Is it??" Anshul said, and raised his eyebrows for my conformation. He was quite observant, I knew. And that was one of the key that made him learn the guitar so finely in such a short span. I nodded.

"Exactly. the 4 A's" Arpit said.

"How about 4 ace's. See each one of us is symbolized by an ace in the deck of cards, making it complete." Ajit said and smirked.

"That sounds good too."

"Yes, but we are forgetting someone. But Payal??" Anshul said, they all looked perplexed.

"Hmmm. What about the fifth one, her name does not even have 'a' as an alphabet??" Ajit said.

"Gottcha, man. The fifth one. So let's call it 'fifth ace'." I thought I had solved our dilemma.

"That's unmistakable, man" Arpit said and smiled at me.

The rest two hi-fived.

The list of the band's participating in the fest, included 1 more new name- MOKSHA. To my astonishment,

MOKSHA was Sameer's band. He succeeded in doing what actually took 3 years of my engineering. But I did not envy him. A bit of shock, but no jealousy I was sure.

Two more bands from other colleges were to perform, so I realized it was not going to be a cake walk for us. On the other hand, VISHESH was not just participating, but also formed a chunk of the main organizer's team for music. Two days before the fest they invited all bands for discussion. Head held high, I entered into the same room I was thrown out of VISHESH two years back. My mind was clouded with all the possible imaginations of what could be lined up before as I walk inside. We all sat, Rohit took the charge. He talked about mics, leads, amps whatever we would be sharing on the stage. Quite unexpectedly, Manav turned up to me with a smiling face. As he started conversing politely, I wondered if I could do any good to him. That tone in which he spoke made me remember of the way he was 3 years ago when we were friends or I assumed that we were so, "Is that ok Aryan, would you like to add anything?".

"Yeah", I reciprocated back the same amity that he displayed.

All eyes turned onto me.

"Actually, we are missing a talk about performance slots",

I said keeping my expressions as calm as possible.

"Yes we have planned that", Manav said looking at Rohit.

"Two bands from other colleges have been allotted first two slots, third slot is for Sameer's band and fourth one is yours". Rohit said, keeping up the suspense, as I rolled myeyes.

"So, your performance is the last one",I said , reflecting sarcasm in my voice. I knew last turn meant an extra benefit to make the performance a big hit.

"yeah, actually…", Manav Said, struggling with words.

"Actually we want to perform in last slot", I said stopping Manav in the mid of his sentence.

Arpit nodded and threw a look at Rohit.

"As we are organizing this event and we are from final year that's why we have decided a last turn for our band", Rohit said.

"Soo, you are organizing this event, does it mean you can decide anything on your own? In that case, even Arpit and I are also from final year".

Silence prevailed for 3-4 seconds.

"If you say, we can talk to Madam in-charge for this", I said with utter confidence.

Manav interrupted to pacify the situation, "Leave it yaar, you can perform at last slot, we have no issues, good performance does not need a specific slot."

I said a mild "okay".

Meeting got wind up in 40 minutes and we came back to our practice room. We had got the last slot to perform, I was happy.

The ultimate day, 30th/march/2011.

Finally, the day I was waiting for had arrived. The crucial day fetched many different feelings aroused inside me. The feelings that I had hardly encountered ever. I simply tossed over bed last night.

In the evening, few minutes before our performance, I could almost hear my heartbeat. VISHESH was performing on stage at that time. I was in no mood to watch their performance. So I kept myself busy in talking with my band mates, checking guitar strings, beholding my dress. Questions were popping up in my mind, making me uneasy every passing second. But, I applaud my senses that helped me.

Suddenly, I received Sirat's phone call. I could not hear her much because of the noise around, I told her and hung up.

She texted me next minute. It said:

"Don't worry. You have done your job, god will now do his. Enjoy the moment you have longed for. Good luck"

I smiled & replied to her "Thanks" is too small a word for you."

We were just about to get called on the stage. I was trying hard to compose myself, pacifying myself that, I was not performing on the stage for the 1st time, so these feelings were not meant to block my way, at any cost. We decided to shuffle Payal's song after 1st two songs by Ajit, So that, we could conclude with the Punjabi rap.

When we went on the stage, it was close to 8:30 pm. I realized I was finally collecting myself to some extent. Music was helping me to gain senses again. It took almost 5 minutes to do the sound check, during which I tried ignoring Manav, Rohit, as much as I could. They both sat on chairs in front row. From the spot I was standing, they were clearly visible. I went to the drummer to give the final commandment a minute before.

As our 20-minutes long performance started, dim blue lights filled the atmosphere. It made every visible thing beautiful by manifolds. The enchanting night, beautifully adorned college, those twinkling lights and cheering faces, life at that moment was so magnificent. Believe me from the top, the audience looked better than all my anticipations.

The dim lights jazzed up as we proceeded further. They pepped us right from the beginning. Even though I was tensed like anything, it helped me play with all my concentration. I had to assure nothing goes wrong.

But with passing moments, things began to seem easy. I was finally on the stage that I have craved from an era. I was finally performing to the people I have been a part from ages. I could see people were enjoying our performance. Music went into action and we obeyed. With every moment, our confidence boosted up, making us do better. Payal's entry made the crowd roar at the top of their voice. She sang well & fulfilled the responsibility given to her. The raps thrilled the audiences. .. The picture perfect lights contributed in making the performance a feast for ears as well as eyes. The songs made the crowd go mad with ecstasy. It was the ultimate view for all of us. The audience pepped us to keep on performing. We had set the stage on fire. Performing to that audience, I was happy that my efforts yielded & brought me up.

The performance went well, by heaven's grace. Just as our performance ended, the crowd demanded "once more".

The announcers asked us to perform one more song

for the compelling audiences. Well, who would not want to?

I approached Ajit to discuss what to perform. I started plucking guitar strings, everybody on stage was speaking whatever was running in their mind.

"Let's add some more action on stage guys, Do you want VISHESH on stage too", one of the announcer announced at the top of her voice.

I screamed at myself "Noooooo!!!!".

In the hustle-bustle I stepped hard on Guitar processor to change the patch and signaled Arpit to give a roll on drums. I started playing random solo Ajit joined too. Fortunately he picked up the correct note. At that moment, I didn't know what I was playing. But whatever it was, I was enjoying and keept saying to myself that I won't let them come on stage. Announcer's voice got muted under my heavy metal base guitar patch. I looked up at the crowd searching for Rohit, Manav. I could not find them anywhere. They were lost among the crowd being just another face in hundreds. Even that made me happy. Destiny had finally made us switch places. If they could see my face, it won't take him much to figure out I was on the top of the world where happiness ruled.

The lights came onto me. It was something, man! I mean, being at the spot light in mid of thousand people. That ray of light was enough to bring one of the widest smiles at my face. I was ECSTATIC.

The lights dimmed and brightened up in nanoseconds. As the performance continued, it gleamed on the rest on our mates and the crowd went at top of its spirits.

And Ajit, the great was gone with the wind. He was shaking his head along with the tone, catching every possible attention. As he came towards my side for crossing the guitars, I dreaded if I would end up laughing my lungs out. The crowd was in love with it. The wobbling of heads spread among them. They were lively as hell. We performed and they roared.

We stepped down from the stage, but I was at the zenith of happiness, a place from where I did not want to return, at least not for a long time. I had fulfilled my wish, my dream. A feeling of content had taken birth in me. I was satisfied, I had finally done it. I went to Pulkit.

"Finallllly... congrats, man." He hugged me.

"Thanks." I was falling short of words.

"Unbelievable!! You guys rocked, it's fun watching your best friend on stage, but you made me feel envious." Pulkit winked.

"Yeahhii. That was the aim of my life." I said and we laughed. Some classmates joined us. I hardly remember the last time, any one of them ever came to me with a wide smile. Today, they were beaming, shaking hands with me.

"That was a great performance, Aryan."

"Yup, never seen something so different in our college."

"Keep it up, man and Ajit was a real hunk!!" just the rapper?? Oh, though I gave an unusual hint but I frankly did not bother. I could not spoil my day.

As I sat there still, my mind replayed the last few moments over and over again. Our performance, those applauses, those praises had made way. The criticism, the disapproval had faded away. I kept on speaking to myself, yes I have done it, yes getting the last slot payed off very well. I didn't let VISHESH to perform in the end. As time passed, the cafe got crowded. I saw some of my acquaintances, they poured blessings,compliments.. They were chameleons, whose opinion mattered to me the least. But I wanted to meet someone, the girl who did not change her mind, who supported me when no one else did. I called Sirat to meet me in the cafeteria.

In less than a minute, she arrived. And I saw her from a distance. Just as she reached, her eyes widened and she said, "Ohh goodness!! What a thrilling performance.

The rapper in your band has such an electrifying stamina, that he has almost exhorted us. " that was all she said.

"Hmm. Yeah." What else could I say her. I was taken aback by what I just heard, what shocked me more was, it was Sirat who had said it.

"What about me?"I wanted to ask her, but I did not.

"Really, his power packed voice was the real icing in your performance." I smiled in a fake manner. Unfortunately, to maintain it was turning out to be tough. I wanted to go away from her.

She talked about every other thing, the fest, the quizzes, her comparing, and our performance. But I had lost interest talking to her. However, I did not want to piss her off, so I kept answering whatever she asked.

I came back, making an excuse that I had to catch up with my classmates. She went off to handle the stage after a while. While watching her announcing on the stage, I wondered how she couldn't find that something was wrong. That something she had done pinched me. But I was sure about one thing if it was said by someone else I would not have bothered that much.

Not this way, I wish

* * *

I expected the night after the fest would be the most peaceful one. However, the expected never happens, at least not in my world. I went through all the things that happened to me in the fateful day. I gained a million things and lost the countless. I fulfilled my desire, my passion. I had an upper hand over those who never thought I'll end up successfully. I had gained content.

But there was a hint of restlessness in a corner of my mind. I could not stop my mind from indulging into the thoughts about Sirat, thoughts that sprung me away from her. How her eyes widened while she was praising Ajit, the moment I met her after my performance. Was she the same girl who had always knew my weak points?? I wondered if she was the same girl who saw me striving for my performance day & night.

I wondered how people could give all the credit to one person while I -worked on it. Maybe that was what made Tushar bother. Maybe these feelings were responsible for making him aggressive with

Kunal. I could now understand, why "VISHESH" got split in the 2nd year fest.

The internal exams after the fest were a catastrophe. For the 1st time, I was least bothered about giving them. I skipped 2 out of 4 exams. And, yes all this seemed usual to us, considering we had reached the final year. I wonder how I could be so mad about the same thing, 3 years ago.

The time to part was approaching, everybody was aware of this. The classrooms started remaining vacated and we began to sit in groups and chit-chat. Something we rarely thought of doing after 1st year, when everyone was everyone's friend. The month of April was at its closing stages.

Sirat called to meet one day. She insisted to give her the treat that I owed her. So, I agreed readily since I had promised her and after all the help that she did, she completely deserved it. This was our first proper meeting after fest. We met in the cafeteria after the college got over. After the treat, we came out to the corridor which was the usual venue for holding all our ad-hoc meetings.

"So tell me something how's college going?? I mean final year, that too about to end??" She asked

"Yeah, seems tough to leave the place. I spend most of the time with my classmates now, no more than 2 classes in a day. I"ll miss the place, i suppose."

"Just the place?? Not the people here??" she asked. "Not really, but maybe someone is an exception." "Who?? Who??" she asked, her eyes lit up.

"My best friend, Pulkit."

"Bet he can't be the only one." She said as I told her a few more names, many of them were the names I hated, that irked me. I finished.

"Ohh." She looked disappointed, as I finished.

"Something wrong with that??"

She moved her neck, saying no. But I could see something was bothering her.

“You’re concealing something. Tell me,“is there something bothering you”??

“Yeah, I guess.” She thought for a couple of minutes and then spoke.

”I think our bond is that strong now, that we can speak our hearts out to each other.” I nodded.

She took a long sigh. “Sir, remember the first time I met you.”

I did remember it well and with years passing by us had brought a sea change between us. That confident girl I saw around 3 years ago wearing blue gloss had become one of my dearest friends.

“Well, the only day you looked innocent to me, madam. “I’m-very-shy” types?? Huh??” I said and laughed. She did too, but only a little. I wondered why she was talking about this. She had always been the one to brush away this topic.

“Yeah, you remember that well, but I was seriously very shy at that moment.”

“Ohoho. How easy is to believe that when I know you this well?” I teased and then added as an afterthought, “things have changed a lot.” I said.

“But something did not.” she kept mum and then spoke again. “My feelings did not. I like you even before I existed for you. From the moment I saw you at my fresher’s eve, I have thought about you. And maybe you know or not, I have never stopped doing it from the past 2 and half years. I just could not.”

That was a kick in my stomach. I did not know what to say. I wished that I was being fooled. Don’t know for how long,

I stared at her hoping if she would laugh out the next moment and say all that she said was a prank or dare or anything but not the truth. She did nothing of that sort.

"Why didn't you tell me this, earlier??"

"But you knew this, sir. I mean it was easy to find out."

"It wasn't, Sirat." I told her. Even if I had the slightest clue about it, I was in no state to tell that to Sirat, at least not then, when she was standing in front of me, pouring her heart out. In those moments, on a couple of occasion when I heard her lines as weird, ran in front of my eyes. Some things which Sirat said as a joke had an undercurrent meaning. I wish I was good enough to understand her subtle ways back then.

"Hmmm.Ok, Let's say, it was not. But now I have told you everything, so??" she said and turned into a stone the next second.

"So what?? What are you expecting now??" I bull-dozed her to speak up. For the first time, making her speak was getting tough.

"What do you expect from the person you like?? You can understand that well." She looked at me hopefully.

"I do. So anything else you want to say" "I don't want you to go."

"Who are you to say that? If you remember, we were just friends." I took a breath, moved my eyes away from hers and then continued speaking.

"I've never known of your intentions. If I had known, then I would not be standing here. I would have never become friends with you." I looked back at her, even her expecting eyes could not stop me from shunning her off. But I was bound to look away. I guess one needs to move the gaze, before breaking someone up. It just gives you the necessary strength which require to do it.

"Sirat, I've just 3 months left to leave the place, so I'm not in a stage to promise you anything. Just because I talk to you, consider you a friend, gives you no right to portray things. There's hardly any future I can see with you, not even in your wildest dreams. Getting??"

I managed to look at her. She was already looking at me, our eyes met. She was about to cry, anyone could easily guess. She wanted to say something, but she did not. Why are you doing all this, I felt like she wanted to ask me. But it was not my mistake. I always considered her as a friend, a very close friend but nothing more than that.

She looked away, just the moment I was going to break the eye-contact.

"What was all that, when you called me your closest friend?? We have been sharing almost every matter over so long." She stood just 3 inches away from my face, as she said that.

"Exactly I'm fond of you as a "friend". it is you who picked me wrong."

"I did. It was a big deal. And trust me sir, you don't even know what you mean to me."

"I don't even want to know." I almost screamed at her and cursed myself the next moment on watching her tremble like that.

"I think I'll walk back." she said, fighting a lump in her throat. I did not stop her and we started walking in the direction of her hostel. There were very few people in the lane, since it was quite late, so I was comfortable performing the custom of seeing her off to the limit. But there was a huge difference today. Titters on her face had got replaced by sobs. The guy responsible for it was walking along her.

Sirat who had been walking, still looking towards the floor,. I did not want to get in to an embarrassing situation.

She understood and her voice broke a little, as she said "I can walk back alone. I don't ..." she kept mum. After a short while, she said, "You can go."

I realized I could not afford to get spotted with a girl, who is a minute short of breaking in to tears. "I'm already going forever." Her heart sank. Our eyes met again. I was struggling to look into them. I said "bye". She did not answer & walked away from me in the direction of her hostel. After a second she left, I looked around to find that it was exactly the same lane I met her for the first time. Things are no longer the same as they were that day. Not even a bit.

Guilt flushed inside me while I made my way back to home. Thoughts of Sirat clouded in my mind, thoughts about the first time I saw her, thoughts about the time that made her my closest friend, and thoughts about the last few minutes when I shattered her without giving a second thought. My heart cramps when I imagined her being pierced. The girl, who just needed half a sentence from me to know that I was upset was reduced to tears. And to the worst, it was me who was responsible for bringing them in her eyes.

May be, if I would have given a second thought, I would not have treated her the way I did. She did not deserve those tears. May be if I would have recalled how she stood by me in ups & downs, how she took chances just to help me in her finals, how she was willing to be on my side every time, how it made a difference to me when she praised someone else, I would not have shoved her away from me. Infinitely away.

I had no other option than bearing the guilt brought by my own actions. I shivered as I imagined her condition when I had left her alone. How could I do that? How could anyone on earth do that?? May be, I should have said a "yes to her". Maybe I should but after a couple of months, or a year when I"ll have to go?? She would have been on the top of the world. But it was just going to be momentary happiness, something that is assured to end. And leaving her after getting that closer would leave a wound much greater than what I gave her that day. I had to win over the soft corner of my heart that I had given to her thoughts. I had to think practically which was good not only for me, but for her too. However if I had one wish granted from god, I would take no time to decide what I want from him. My only wish is to erase that one day from my life. The moment of ill-luck that snatched an angel from me.

"Ohh, but we can't blame all of it on her." Pulkit said, as he came to know about Sirat.

I threw him a look, strange enough to make him understand that he should not weigh up our faults, sitting in the ivory tower.

"Now what?" He asked as he tries to restart the conversation.

I shrugged and took a long sigh.

"Ok, let's face the truth man. Look Aryan, this is between two of us, so tell me the truth. Do you like her?"

Taken aback, I made the sorest kind of expression I can, "Of course not, and of all the people on this planet, you are asking me this question? Had it been the case, I would have told you beforehand, man."

"I know, but now that you're behaving this silent, anybody could suspect that."

"Suspect what?"

"Those feelings for her have aroused in you. I think so…"

"You are free to think whatever pleases you." I said cutting him, amid of his sentence, irked by his last statement.

"Ok, calm down. Did you guys talk after that?" Pukit said, with an expression one cannot shun easily. I really did not have to be ruthless with every person alive. I tried to calm myself down, as the last I wanted to happen now was watch him walk out.

"She did not call. And so did I." I said and then added as an afterthought, "To make some distance." I guess, I needed to tell the reason to myself more than that to Pulkit.

"After she told you all this, you hate her, don't you?"

"I don't know." I said without paying any second

thoughts. I could not hate her. In the frame of my manipulative mind, I still felt Sirat was a kid, who was just infatuated. A corner of my heart asked if infatuations could survive for as long as 3 years.

"Hmmm. So, you don't love her neither do you hate her, man? At least make it clear what you want."

"I don't know, I mean I wish we could remain friends like we used to be."

"Oh c'mon, stop acting like a girl wanting to cling to this"friends forever" notion. Either let her go or."

"Or screw her? Huh?"

"That's not how I meant it, Aryan. And you know that well." I did, but I was in a mess not to think wise at that point of time. It was funny that I was feeling creepy as if I was the one who fell for Sirat, and not her.

"I'm sorry."

"It's ok. You just need to admit the fact that these things could happen to anyone."

"Yeah, but why her? Pulkit, I know it was not her fault. But how am I supposed to react when one of my best friends admits that she fell for me years back. I'm the last one to know about it. I'm not fortunate enough to keep her by side, just because I don't want to leave her shattered after a year or so. She turns out to be totally frail, breaking herself down and making me feel guilty. And, what I'm left to do in the end? Watch her walk away?" I said and then added, "Just because I can't get on to this long distance kind of crap. Nobody does. This relationship would have got her nowhere we both know. How do I shut my eyes to that?" Hearing my words, Pulkit shrugged. Though I expected him to speak, but he did not say a word.

Some days later, I met Ajit in the college. He waved at me. It took me a bit than the usual to recognize whether his new hairdo was the result of a pitfall made by the stylist or Mr. rapper's own idea.

"Here we go, the new hairstyle. Ahem ahem." I said, making a dig at him.

"Nice, isn't it?? It took me almost half-an-hour to explain this to the guy." He said, bragging his new look. In fact, his accent appeared quite transformed. Now where was that coming from?? Hollywood, I guess.

Nice???? Tough question!! But I hid my smile and nodded at him. I realized he was on cloud nine that day.

"Ohh, so tell me how many proposals have you received??" I asked him.

"Actually, I have stopped counting now." "Really????"

"Yeah. Wonder if girls have something else to do here than just day-dreaming." He continued to blow his own trumpet. And his expressions while saying that were making me laugh. But I tried to control & compose an expression to appear really sympathetic towards the new post-fest rockstar".

"Anyways, I'll catch you later sir, I need to go. Bbbyyee. " "Sure. Bye." He left. Thank god, now I could at least laugh.

Our last semester at college was much alike the very 1st one in the sense that now most of the groups of our entire class has fused into each other, forgetting every rift. I guess it was because of the grim realization that the time of our parting was not far. I was fooling around with my classmates in the cafeteria when I saw Sirat.

The last I met her was 9 days ago. It was the same day that I broke her heart. That was the 1st time I saw her after that. Though, she could not see me, but from my point of view she was fairly visible. Or maybe she was trying to ignore looking around so that she could not find her culprit. Sirat had come over with her classmates, but rarely in those 10 minutes, I saw her talking to anyone of them. After a couple of more minutes, her gaze fell upon me. I was already looking at her. To say the least, she looked the same way as I had left her 9 days ago.

I was expecting my presence to get acknowledged but she lowered eyes without reacting much. I was guilt-ridden on watching her doing that. With every passing minute, I had a sudden urge to walk up to her. An inexplicable urge to explain myself to her. An urge to ask her why was she being such a kid and where the hell she had lost that contagious smile. And to tell her that, to hell, it still mattered to me. There are more things important in life. I wished I could make her understand. But I could not afford to create more issues for her.

Fortunately, a few moments later Sirat looked at me again. This time, her expression little softened. Battling against my ruthless mind, I picked up my cell-phone and gave up my ego, and texted her:

"I hope I don't look that scary, but you tell me do I?"

I saw Sirat checking her phone the next moment, but she did not care to answer me back. I wondered what was so captivating on the floor of the cafeteria as her eyes riveted to it. I mean, she really did not have to think like I had put up a million dollar question. She cared to reply me back but after 5 long minutes.

"No."

Unfortunately, those five minutes were enough to make my mood go upside down, hitting my ego, to boil me up. A million things were running in my mind to write back to her but I ended up writing just 6 words:

"Can't you forget all that happened?"

"That would be like turning my face from harsh reality. Please, don't expect anything of that sort from me, Sir."

"Then accept the reality. Look at yourself, Sirat. You're ruining it for yourself."

"I'm not. Sir, can you please stop making this more difficult? I'm left too behind to do that. You don't worry, I

can handle my life."

Honestly, reading those words, my world blacked out for a second.

"Do as you wish." I finally wrote back. My eyes met her face before I came out of the cafeteria.

Even the moments of our fresher's party were fidget fresh in my mind, when I heard the news that our farewell party had been decided in "Hotel Modesty" on 7th may 2011, as it was decided by our juniors. The last party of my engineering stood there right next to me. How fast time flies in front of one's eyes. I could not stop the time. No one could. But I wanted to make it memorable for myself.

One evening when I was busy making choices about my apparel, Nikhil called me up. He was a year junior to me. But I had known him for years, since we were in the same school.

He said "A guy called Manav is disturbing the preparations we have made for the "farewell".

"How come?? What does he want??" I asked him.

"Actually, he has collected 7-8 other people from the final year and just 3 days before the party, they are demanding for a change the venue to Hotel C.R.. We would have tried but we have already made some advance payments to the "Hotel Modesty". So it has ended up in a huge fuss."

"Hmm, but hotel modesty was chosen because it was a way better than C.R."

"Uhm, and almost all of your classmates had given their consent to that, on Friday. But now they are turning their back off." Nikhil said, as a matter-of-fact.

"Ohh I see. Have you guys tried to sort it out one-on-one with him??"

"We have tried more than once, but he's being too adamant. I thought to talk to some senior who could help us. So, you were the first name in my mind."

"I see you have a right point and don't worry, nobody wants their farewell party to get spoilt, so hopefully they might not mind bending a bit."

I hung up the phone & thought what was meant to be done. Manav was never a friend of mine, but Tanya's love for him along his ways in the past was enough to make him adore the list of "my silent rivals". So, calling him up would mean a squirm on my ego. But I could not let him do everything the way likes, so I found his contact number and called him up. After a bit of normal "hi-how are you" chat, I asked him for what I called him.

"Why do you want the farewell to be held at C.R. instead of Hotel Modesty??" yes, I admit hating every inch of him but while asking this question, I took special care of my tone. I kept it polite.

In the last few days, I did not want to get remarked as rude by any one. I wanted to make the ending of my engineering "pleasant" for others. , I was always nasty to many of them. Of course, that was only my preference over being pretentious.

"Ohh, but it's just not me now. I have talked with many of our friends who want the venue to be altered. You have a problem with that??" towards the end of his statement, his tone had become quite contradictory to mine.

"Not me, but those who have organized the party have."

"You mean our juniors."

Of course, who else would I mean by that, the house-keeping department of "hotel Modesty"??

"Yeah. Actually, they have already paid some share of the payment ...." I was speaking when I heard the tone of my phone. The last call cost message flashed, indicating the phone call got disconnected.

Ahh, these network errors have such a perfect timings, I thought to myself. And I dialed his number again. This time, he disconnected the phone without even picking it up. I understood that it was not the networks issue for the call's abrupt cut off. Rather, Manav was sick enough to be blamed for running off. Bloody coward.

Half an hour later, I texted a message to him:

"We'll do the party where it has been decided. Stop it if you can."

He replied back:

"Listen you f#%! # me&^#@ , it would be better if you s#i^% stay out. Bl#$%%. . Swear......... "*

After a minute, I received another one. He was such a pimp. I wanted to come back with the f*#!in bastard in his own language, but I controlled my anger. I decide not to rebut, not to abuse him back. It was not the best time to answer. I kept my patience. I knew I would get a better time to teach him a lesson. Eager I was, but I waited for the right occasion to come.

Next day in the college, Computers-3rd year and 4th year students assembled in the cafeteria to resolve the matter. We came to know that Manav had managed to plot & persuade a majority of hostellers to get on his side, in just one night. I had become insensitive to this, after spending years in a class full of unreliable hostellers.

In the morning, Nikhil and his friends had requested me to stand by them. I told them that I would not step back from my words and I'll try to convince my classmates thoroughly.

When I saw Manav, I blistered with fury within. Tanya like always was being the backbone of her sweetheart. But I tried to divert my attention by talking to Pulkit & the juniors. After sometime, the moment came when I had to confront him, talk to him face to face. I kept my point against him. In his air, he hardly paid any heed to my words. He interrupted in between, but I stopped him bluntly, asking him to wait till I completed.

When he was asked to speak, he preferred yelling. What else is expected from people who can't quote significant explanations for their useless demands?

It would not be wrong, if he was titled as the most annoying creature. Just as I turned back to leave the place, he caught hold of my right wrist all of a sudden and gave me a jerk. He must have not expected how much he would have to pay for that action of his. Before a moment would pass, I pulled out my left hand and placed a tight slap on his right cheek. I made sure that I should make that one, as hard as possible. Quite unexpectedly, he fell off to the direction of my hand.

Seeing that some teachers gathered around, a sudden hustle-bustle got uproar in the cafeteria. I'm sure if anyone of them had caught hold of me, it would have resulted in guaranteed pack-up from the college that day. Pulkit & Nikhil who were standing behind me pulled me back. Away from the situation. While I was being pulled back, I glanced at her. Sirat stood at a distance, looking at me in fret. Even in a crowd of a hundred, I could recognize her. But before I managed to make out something else, she got off my sight.

The most enjoyable slap I could deliver not only insulted Manav, but also made the junior girls go mad with worry. For a moment, they thought of backing out from the farewell party. Though, it involved giving them stretched assurance, but somehow the matter got suppressed.

After two -and a half hour, I decided to talk to some of my brainy classmates to negotiate a solution. I talked to everyone and tried hard to convince them courteously.

I even told them that hardly anyone from 3rd year was willing to attend the party at "Hotel C.R". I told them it would bring them a loss of thousands. And that the farewell without juniors would mean just a simple get-together. But they did not see eye to eye with me. Like always.

People whom I called "friends" for the last four years, people whom I never said "no" to, people whom I helped in every situation I could, did not agree to me. They were too inflexible to compromise, to adjust. They chose "Hotel C.R." as the venue for the "farewell"party.

That eve, I texted Sirat. "Were you present in the cafeteria??"

She replied. "Yeah, it was me. I saw you from a distance."

"Oh. So will you be attending the farewell??" I wrote the question that was bothering me & send it to her.

"No. I too was on your side." In hearts of my hearts, her answer contented me. It meant a lot.

"Ok." She did not reply after that.

The next day, Pulkit asked me to pay the money for farewell party.

"Have you gone mad??" I asked him.

"Since the day I found you in life. But what is it now??"

"Pulkit, how can I go for this "farewell"?? I do suppose I have some self-respect existing inside me."

"Look Aryan, I know you are taking sides but it is our farewell party!! Do you even realize we have been waiting for this? Even you were so keen, so now how do you expect us to miss this??"

"Excuse me, I'm not going & I'm not asking you to stay. You are making me angry now."

He kept mum, when I added. "Feel free to do what your heart says."

"Thanks a lot for your permission, sir." Disgust was written all over Pulkit's face.

"Anything else??" I said, as he walked out.

Though, it took one complete day for my thick-head

to realize that I was being extra rude to Pulkit, that too where he was no were fault at. But when this fact finally registered my mind, I wasted no more time to call him up. After 2 minutes of uncomfortable one-sided conversation, i made up my mind and said:

"I'm sorry, man. I should not have spilled beans on you yesterday. I'm really guilty about it."

"Oh shut up you idiot, and for god's sake stop sounding like you are apologizing to your girlfriend." He said and laughed, thinking of my stupidity.

"So, is the suit ready??" I asked.

"Which suit??"

"The one you gave for stitching for the farewell party."

"Ohh that one. I've changed my mind."

"Why?? That suit was nice."

"No, about the farewell."

"Are you kidding me?? But why????" I felt guilty.

"I guess, they'll be able to do without me. But how have I enjoyed without my only friend's company."

We did what I had never thought of. We missed our own farewell. Pulkit missed his farewell for me. He was one crazy guy I could rarely find any competition for. Most of the past few years, I had hated him for giving me a bit say in the things that primarily belonged to me, but now that I see back, I find myself lucky to have this jerk in my life.

I was satisfied to do what my conscience told me. For me, my "ego" was prior to the festivity. Most of the juniors too stayed at their words by not attending the farewell, which had now got restricted into a get-together.

My heart had given it up from my classmates. A mere thought of their faces even began to annoy me. Some of them even apologized to me after the party. But it hardly made any difference to me. The way they snubbed me, when I asked them for support had left an imprint on my mind.

Exams started within no time. The 4-subject course went like a walk in the park, short & easy. On the day of the last exam, I could smell the politeness in the air. My classmates were the category of people who never failed to surprise me. I could not have expected my classmates to be so warm till that day was held. When I was hating to see those sore faces, I found them screaming for amity. And I was dumbstruck by what I got, sheer friendliness. I mean, were those smiles for real?

If they are not saints, they are not really wicked. A few of them not at all wicked. I kept this repeating in my mind. The grudges replaced with embraces, even if it was for just one day. We resembled like siblings (Couples excuse!) who had reunited after life-long partitions.

And all of a sudden, all the good times that we had shared on this part of the planet clouded my mind, putting all the frictions into shade.

After 4 days, one of my classmates called me and asked to come to the college. It was time for hostellers to depart. I refused to go back to them, who did not even deserve a good-bye in my sight.

The college ended on 20th June 2011.

Back at home, the first 4-5 days, it felt quite similar to the way it was around 4 years ago. When after I had wrapped up with my Twelfth exams, that same relaxation, the monotonous idleness and the long wait. Then I was waiting for my college life to begin & now I was waiting for my career to get a start. The days were the longest I had ever seen. And that was when time hardly seemed to move. Boredom definitely has the potential to drive one crazy. Silently perhaps. Courtesy to mom's comments that

I received every morning, I realized it was not the moon yet. I started utilizing time in brushing up my general knowledge by hanging onto various news channels.

Amidst of all this, there was one thing that I never left behind, music. I could survive without food for days, but music was my oxygen, my rehab, and not a mere stand-by. When I wanted to talk to someone and my contacts seemed in dearth, I picked up my guitar. It never gave me a "no". When I was bored & restless, I choose playing keyboard. Music was the icing on my plain cake. It soothed me in every moment of discomfort.

Life had come to standstill but lucky enough, I had received my joining letter from TCS before I thought I would be overcome by Idleness.

"Joining date: July 29, 2011 & Venue: Ahmadabad".

After a few minutes, Pulkit told me that we shared the joining date & the venue as well. It made me feel better. A lot better.

I had finally entered the month when I'll be joining my job. The month that would take me away from here, the month that would transport me to another state, a city that I had never seen before. The Month that I had been waiting for so long.

Meanwhile, mom at home announced that I should start collecting things now. I began shopping with her, to Get the requirements. I was going to join the corporate world. So, it meant that I could not hang around my office, wearing my denim jeans & tees. It was time to make formals wear a way of life. I had to buy shirts, and trousers. Like every other guy, I hated shopping, but I could not run away this time. She said that she did not want me to make any compromises. I brought the other necessities too. Shoes, sleepers, 1 blanket, prescribed medicines, everything. A month passed in shopping, showing faces to my kith and Kin, and arranging documents that were to be taken along.

Finally, the ultimate day arrived when I will be leaving for my job, standing outside the Delhi Airport with my Parents

I checked my phone there was a new message , from Sirat.

It said:

"Best of luck to my fav. guitarist :) Wish that smile always remains. Otherwise here I'm to bring it back :)" I replied her:

"Thanks a lot :) p.s. : I'm in roaming :P :D t.c."

I saw mom struggling with her bag. Her fastest ever.

"I had forgotten to get these, son." Mom said as she handled me what she had shopped. She had brought a wallet & some handkerchiefs. Both for me.

"Nothing for you."

"I needed these only. Put your first salary into the new one." I stood there raising my eyebrows. So, she added "it's lucky. Kids don't get it." oh ya kid, I resigned to her orders.

"yup, I would."

"And call us the moment....."

I interrupted her in between "us the moment you reach Ahmadabad & the moment you find your place and every day twice. See mom, I have learnt it by heart." We busted in to pangs of laughter.

The announcement was made. I had to go for check-in.

"Ohh.. Take care of yourself." Mom said.

"I'll, you too take care."

"And eat properly." She reminded.

"I promise."

I looked at dad. He was smiling now. His eyes said, I'll look after your mom. They spoke even if he could not.

"You also take care of yourself." I told dad.

"Yes dear" he replied. I smiled. My parents meant a world to me. My love could never blur for them, no matter how far I go. After the call, they embraced me and waved a goodbye. I touched their feet and came in the check-in section. They went back home.

Epilogue

* * *

In the end, I am falling short of words or may be running away from the truth. Everything seems so small, the efforts I had put up to form a band, those clashes does that mean anything now. We all will be in different world and a rare chance of seeing each other's face. A million thoughts cloud my mind and I shuttle back & forth. Questions get sprinted in my head.

Did I need to prove anything to someone?

Who I did this for?

Does this make a difference to me now?

What if destiny didn't allow me to perform?

Was something necessary still left for me to do?

Is there anyone who still remembers the time I performed?

There is only one answer:

"Yes, I did this "**FOR THE SAKE OF MY EGO**".